Also from Indigo Sea Press

By Odell Myers

The Irreversible Life of Mann

indigoseapress.com

For Heaven's Sake

The e-mails of St. Peter, Gatekeeper

By

Odell Myers

Deep Indigo Books
Published by Indigo Sea Press
Winston-Salem

Deep Indigo Books
Indigo Sea Press
302 Ricks Drive
Winston-Salem, NC 27103

First Deep Indigo Books edition published January, 2016

Deep Indigo Books, Moon Sailor and all production design are trademarks of Indigo Sea Press, used under license.

For information regarding bulk purchases of this book, digital purchase and special discounts, please contact the publisher at indigoseapress.com

Cover design by Stacy Castanedo

Manufactured in the United States of America
ISBN 978-1-63066-417-6

Odell Myers

FOREWORD

A glitch similar to crosstalk in old telephone systems or a geomagnetic storm's widespread interference with electronic systems might account for these e-mails. They purport to document the posthumous career of a famous but often legendary figure. Their format is virtually the same as e-mails on earth's Internet. Minor variations are self-explanatory.

***

"And I say also unto thee, That
thou art Peter, and upon this rock
I will build my church; and the gates
of hell shall not prevail against it.
"And I will give unto thee the
keys of the kingdom of heaven; and
whatsoever thou shalt bind on earth
shall be bound in heaven; and whatsoever thou shalt loose on earth
shall be loosed in heaven."

(Matthew 16: 18-19. The Bible (King James Version)

1

From: "SIMONPETER" <sptr4/12gtkpr@etrnl.hvn>;
"P.SIMON" <psm_48@ppt.spl>;
To: "THE CHIEF" <*******@etrnl.hvn>; "JC"
<jchrst@etrnl.hvn>;
Cc: "MANAGEMENT" <ORGmgmnt1=3@etrnl.hvn>;
"ANDY" <adrw6/12@etrnl.hvn>; "MATT"
<mtthw1/12fnnc@etrnl.hvn>;
"HQ FINANCE" <hqfnc@etrnl.hvn>; "PAUL"
<pl13/12@etrnl.hvn>;
"JOHN" <jnz2/12hqhhmnrscrs@etrnl.hvn>; "SPRTS"
<EXkr@etrnl.hvn>;
"HQ HUMAN RESOURCES" <hqhmnrsrcs@etrnl.hvn>;
"JIM—ED & ENT" <jms3/12@etrnl.hvn>; "DRLUKE"
<drlk@etrnl.hvn>;
"BART" <brt7/12whlns@etrnl.hvn>; "SECURITY"
<scrty@etrnl.hvn>;
"MAINTENANCE" <mntnc@etrnl.hvn>; "B"
<BlzB@othrsd.prm>;
"WREN" <srcwrn@etrnl.hvn>; "HQ"
<cnstrtn&rpr@tmprl.lmb>

Sent:wzk02

Subject: Folder entitled wx29–wzp Containing My E-mails &
TTXMessages (Attached)

I have reached a decision that I tremble to reveal. But here
goes: I request permission to emigrate from Heaven. Since my
reasons for this unprecedented request developed over several
soul-searching earth-centuries, they will be incomprehensible
unless you know all of the facts. FYI, therefore, I have
compiled all of the relevant correspondence in the subject
folder.

For Heaven's sake, please read all of it before ruling on my
request. I have tried in vain to find another solution.

Respectfully and Urgently.—Simon Peter, Gatekeeper
Emeritus

Odell Myers

From: "SIMONPETER" <sptr4/12gtkpr@etrnl.hvn>
To: "ANDY" <adrw6/12@etrnl.hvn>

Sent:wx29

Subject: Help!

Help, Brother! I never thought I could be unhappy in Heaven but I am and it's driving me crazy. It's disloyal. But I can't help it. And I want a transfer or a new assignment.

In a lengthy and almost incredible comedy of errors, the Powers that Be got caught up in a modernization frenzy and, in the name of efficiency, they successively reduced the Entrance Section work force to exactly one man—ME! Since that day of infamy, I have been on my feet at The Gate without a real break for a little over 200 earth years. And millions of people are stuck in Limbo, waiting to find out whether they have made it to Heaven or The Other Side.

So please do me a favor: Casually mention to JC that I might be interested in another assignment. Be diplomatic. Act as though you are just wondering whether or not a change of scenery would be good for me. Whatever you say, don't blurt out that I'm stuck in a dead-end job that's inferior to the one he gave me on earth and that no one man in Heaven or on earth can do the job that I am expected to do. Soften him up a bit, Brother. And let me know his reaction so I can figure out what to do next. –Simon

From: "ANDY" <<u>adrw6/12@etrnl.hvn</u>>
To: "SIMONPETER" <<u>sptr4/12gtkpr@etrnl.hvn</u>>

Sent:wx31

Subject: FW "Help." (Ref. only.)

Slow down, Simon! I can't bother JC just because you're
fed up with your job. Especially since the problem you
mentioned occurred 200 years ago! If I dropped that on him, he
would have you picked up by ambulance and rushed to
emergency! Sounds to me like you just need a vacation. But
let's talk.

(Switch to TTX)

ANDY I'm worried about you, Simon, because reacting to
something 200 years after the fact is not normal, even for
someone as high strung as you. So what's really bugging you?
SIMONPETER Modernization's the problem and it's been
bugging me a lot longer than 200 years. I wish I had never
heard of the word. I'm dead certain—excuse the expression—
that modernization's the straw that broke the camel's back.
ANDY You're overreacting, Simon. Have you forgotten what
life was like back in Galilee: If you think those were the good
old days, you are sick. And I mean sick!
SIMONPETER Who's talking about Galilee?
Modernization's a heavenly problem that wiped out the most
important difference between heaven and earth. Deleted it!
Zapped it! All because heaven imported more ideas from earth
than vice versa, creating a creeping brain gain that began
innocently enough but picked up incredible speed with Johann
Gutenberg's arrival in 1468 CE. I remember welcoming him—
a seedy looking, bearded chap with long legs protruding like
stilts out of those ridiculous bloomers men wore then.
Admitting him took a little extra time because he went by the
name of Johann Gutenberg (John Beautiful Mountain) instead

4

of his birth name—Johann Gensfleisch. Can't blame him for changing it. Imagine going through life as John Gooseflesh! **ANDY** Sit down and take a deep breath, brother! Sounds like you're hyperventilating! And no wonder: First you talk about what happened 200 years ago, then you up it to 500 years! But who is Johann Gutenberg and what does he have to do with you?

SIMONPETER That's what I'm trying to tell you. Until Gutenberg arrived, heaven had been a cozy place. When we arrived, I immediately took over as Gatekeeper, an assignment that I had welcomed on earth without realizing its celestial implications. Nevertheless, I got right to work and quickly recruited an enthusiastic staff—linguists fluent in all languages, librarians who cataloged and indexed the scrolls and ponderous books of life, competent monitors who maintained order.

ANDY I wish you'd stick to the subject, Simon, instead of wandering down memory lane.

SIMONPETER Modernization's the subject in case you've forgotten and I'm stuck with it, no matter how I sound. Stick with me so you can explain it to JC. Early on, the Gatekeeper was essentially a welcoming host because the Judgment Seat was in operation. It was the first big casualty of modernization even before Gutenberg arrived. Once Lawyers showed up, they quickly inundated the Court with an endless list of demands and objections like discovery, change of venue, police brutality, not guilty because of temporary insanity, immaturity, childhood abuse, insufficient evidence, etc.

ANDY I was there when the Tribunal shut down but I don't remember your agonizing over it. So what's the big deal now?

SIMONPETER You don't remember because I was never the complaining type. When the responsibility fell on me like a rockslide, I just took over where the Tribunal left off. No time for judgment: If your name was in the book, you were in. Otherwise, off to The Other Side. Members of my staff deserve hero medals! Even though our workload fluctuated with a steady succession of wars, crusades, epidemics, inquisitions, tsunamis, earthquakes, tornados, hurricanes and volcanic eruptions, we operated on a first come, first served basis before so-called efficiency experts invented the term FIFO. Surely you remember my nice little room above the Gate where you and other friends dropped in for a cup of tea, some smoked fish and dates. Not on the Sabbath, of course, because I then closed the Gate and did no work.

ANDY I almost envied you then because you were in charge of an entire department and I as yet had no permanent assignment. But please get to the point, Simon. So far, you've told me nothing that's worth bothering JC.

SIMONPETER Hold your horses, Andy. If I don't tell you the whole story, none of it will make sense. I must have showed you the Library because I was so proud of it. There's something about thousands of scrolls in orderly pigeon holes and books on shelves and the rich organic smell of leather, old papyrus and inks. The sights and smells gripped me in ways that only a man of ancient letters can appreciate. Showing off my Library, however, was a big mistake because Matt and John dropped by one day, all excited about a new arrival named Gutenberg.

ANDY Well finally! The famous Gutenberg appears on stage!

SIMONPETER Don't be flippant, Andy. I really am in trouble and I need your help. Have you any idea how it feels to be unhappy in Heaven? I hate to think what will happen to me if I go off halfcocked. At the Gate, I am too close to The Other Side to act nonchalant about making a mistake!

ANDY Sorry, brother, but your tale of woe so far isn't exactly overflowing with woe! But maybe you're getting warm so I will try to hold my tongue.

SIMONPETER Thanks! Anyway, Matt and John were all charged up about Gutenberg. "On earth," John said, "he revolutionized dissemination, storage and retrieval of information by inventing a practical printing press that used moveable type. His invention put the scribes that used to torment us out of business!"

"In no time," Matt exclaimed, "Each person on earth can have a Bible of his or her very own and free Bibles will be available in each room in every inn in the world."

"This library," John's sweeping gesture covered every precious scroll and book I had, "is already obsolete. We talked it over with The Chief and he agreed that it should be modernized. Gutenberg already is recruiting and training a task force to get the project underway."

I'm not technically educated so many of these modern terms went right over my head without ringing any bells. But Matt and John were all steamed up and ready to go, full speed ahead. So I hate to cut this short because applicants waiting for processing are getting pretty impatient. If it's ok with you, I will send the rest of the story by e-mail. Please, please don't mention my problems to JC until you know the complete story. **ANDY** I can hardly wait is an overstatement but I guess I have no choice. I'll wait.

From: "SIMONPETER" <sptr4/12gtkpr@etrnl.hvn>
To: "ANDY" <adrw6/12@etrnl.hvn>

Sent:wx36

Subject: Modernization Continued

Maybe your remote assignments have shielded you from modernization although our recent conversation indicated that you may be contaminated with its virus-like effects! A sure sign is the expectation that anything worth saying can be said in a 30-second sound bite. I wish it were that simple! But modernization works like whatever spoils fish when you take it out of water. And I guess you remember how that smells!

Do you ever miss those days when we were just a couple of youngsters fishing on Galilee before JC stopped by and said *Come on, I'll show you how to catch men?* I remember even though nostalgia is about the last thing anyone here thinks about. But back to Gutenberg and his project to modernize my library—a project that I heard about after Matthew and John had already cleared it with The Chief.

"Gutenberg is something else," John said. On his office wall is a large Project Control Chart that schedules each step and labels some steps as bottlenecks. He promises that the Project will be completed correctly and on time. You don't have to lift a finger, Pete.

"The Task Force will print obsolete records and place them in permanent storage. Current records will be printed in uniform-sized volumes and arranged alphabetically by language and placed on shelves in revolving carousels. Index cards cross-referenced every which way imaginable will be instantly accessible in horizontal roller files. Your department's efficiency index will hit the roof!" Well, they left me with a headache from grappling with all those new terms—task force... project... schedules... bottlenecks... carousels... efficiency index.... However, the project sounded intriguing and I naively volunteered my best linguists for the Task Force.

Odell Myers

And Project Manager Gutenberg took those bottlenecks in stride, met every deadline and delivered a turnkey job. The new Library was a beauty and our efficiency index indeed hit the roof. My linguists and scribes spent most of their time playing Chaturanga (the predecessor of chess) and the more ancient board games of GO and Senet yet we processed applicants so quickly that the backlog virtually disappeared.

The Chief sent me an embossed and personally signed letter formally promoting me to The Gatekeeper. What an honor! Immediately, I had the letter framed and I displayed it on the wall of my accustomed workstation where every applicant for entry into heaven could see it. If anyone questioned my authority, I simply pointed to the letter and that was that!

✽ ✽ ✽ ✽ ✽ ✽

FA52

SIMON PETER
THE GATE

DEAR SIMON:

WITH GREAT PLEASURE, I AM
ANNOUNCING YOUR PROMOTION
TO CHIEF EXECUTIVE OFFICER OF
THE NEWLY-TITLED ENTRANCE
SECTION.

YOU MAY, IF YOU PREFER, STILL
USE YOUR OLD TITLE—THE
GATEKEEPER.

THANK YOU FOR A JOB WELL DONE.

THE CHIEF

CC: STAFF

Soon after clearing the backlog in Limbo, a flurry of printed organization announcements began arriving in my mailbox. Matthew became head of a FINANCIAL SECTION that included PURCHASING; John headed a brand new

For Heaven's Sake

PERSONNEL SECTION. Before the ink was dry on the announcements, these new SECTIONS stirred up a literal storm of paperwork requiring immediate response.

Personnel sent a 6-page Experience, Education and Aptitude Inventory form that I had to fill out for everyone in my SECTION. Before that was completed, a raft of a 4-page Performance Review forms arrived and I had to evaluate each employee and establish performance objectives for the next period.

FINANCE, not to be outdone, got in the act with a 12-page Budget form that was overdue when it arrived! LEGAL, too, put in its oar in the form of a 225-page Organization Procedures Manual.

Once the various SECTIONS discovered printing and different type fonts, they went wild with colored paper in different paper sizes and exotic fonts. Each section tried to outdo the other and many of them, especially PERSONNEL, hired graphic artists to give their stationery and forms a professional and distinctive touch. After the computer network was deployed, ordinary e-mails written in colored type and illustrated like sales brochures would show up. Bandwidth meant absolutely nothing and it took earth years and the creation of an INFORMATION TECHNOLOGY SECTION (IT) to curb the misuse of the network

In the early years after Gutenberg's arrival, it was, excuse the expression, hell! Filling out forms and trying to organize the blizzard of odd-sized paper kept me so busy that our efficiency index dropped into the cellar and expired! I had no time to read the Procedures Manual but the subtitle was *Internal* so I probably didn't miss much.

Meanwhile at The Gate, the queue again had lengthened and the monitors were unable to maintain order. All they could do was block The Gate and let one applicant at a time squeeze past. Nevertheless, the forms finally were in the mail and my entire staff and I heaved sighs of relief and tried to make up for lost time. Then the axe fell in the form of an official PERSONNEL form letter that outdid itself in snippy,

Odell Myers

bureaucratic prose. It obviously was composed during
PERSONNEL'S s *blue* period!

PERSONNEL SECTION

FB23
Simon Peter
Chief Executive Officer
The Entrance Section

Dear Mr. Peter:

*It has been determined that the
Entrance Section is overstaffed by
66.6%. Sufficient pink slips are
enclosed to downsize the Section,
effective immediately.*

*Affected personnel are directed to
report to the Personnel Section for
evaluation and possible retraining.
Personnel eligible for early retirement
will be encouraged to accept a
generous severance package.*

*All affected personnel are assured
that every effort will be made to
minimize the impact of this necessary
force reduction.*

For the Personnel Section

Finance then added insult to injury by requiring
resubmission of the Budget form to reflect the downsized
Entrance Section.
Amazing! When Heaven imports a revolutionary idea from
earth, it implements the idea and its ramifications at a pace
impossible to achieve on earth. Heaven just pulls out all the

11

For Heaven's Sake

stops and goes for it! Herr Gutenberg led the pack. Obviously, he kept right on thinking and his head was full of unfinished business. (I may be using a few terms that actually came later but old Johann actually lit the fuse that blew what he called our "antiquated notions" to smithereens!)

Heaven raced from his primitive printing press to 4-color offset presses long before they appeared on earth. As modernization picked up speed, a wide range of office equipment followed in its wake.

(Switch to TTX)

ANDY Stop right there, Simon! In my entire existence, I never heard so many strange words as the load you're laying on me without catching your breath. What is a 4-color offset press? A fuse? An office? Ramification? Budget? Even the words computer and e-mail are confusing, although I gather they have something to do with how we communicate. For your information, I hear every message you send in Aramaic and reply in Aramaic, the same language we spoke when we were kids. I could read your name and mine but not much else and the technical words can't be translated. They come through loud and clear in original form.

For heaven's sake, brother, the people here are still using stone tools. JC and I each have a stone knife whose handle houses a tiny communicator of some sort. When you send a message, it vibrates silently. If I'm with someone, I can stop it and play back your message later when I am alone. So, please, explain a few things or I will have to give up and ignore at least half of what you seem to be telling me!

SIMONPETER If I stop and try to educate you on technology, we'll never get anywhere. I still don't understand all of the technical terms, but I can use things like a computer. It's just a tool, like a very smart stylus and, like a scribe, I can write with it on paper instead of vellum. It's not much different from talking or listening to the handle of a stone knife! Even so, I will do my best to avoid technical terms so you won't be confused. By the way, they usually are in English, a sort of universal language on earth today. Heaven just adopted it!

Heaven pretty well skipped the heavy parts of earth's industrial revolution and I managed to weather the continuous paper storms although they almost drove me crazy. The Entrance Section endured additional downsizing and my staff had dwindled to three assistants and me when Sir Isaac Newton arrived in 1727 CE and launched the granddaddy of all modernization.

Barely inside Heaven, he demanded information on the whereabouts of famous men like Archimedes, Euclid, Leonardo da Vinci, Galileo, Pascal, Kepler, Descartes, etc.

Soon he had established a Think Tank, the first in Heaven's history. And as earth time passed, he kept adding the outstanding scientists in every discipline, giants like Einstein and practical inventors like George Washington Carver and Thomas Edison.

ANDY You just yanked me out of the kettle and threw me into the fire! Who are all these people? Seems to me that you are just name dropping. Next thing I hear, you will be bragging about an audience with Caesar or the High Priest.

SIMONPETER I'm not bragging. These people are important because they are part of the brain-gain that modernized heaven. They brought with them the technology, the know-how to make all sorts of tools for the benefit of mankind, even us primitives who were here before them.

Sir Isaac Newton, for example, was one of the most influential men in human history—a physicist, mathematician, astronomer, theologian, alchemist, philosopher. Excuse the technical terms, but take my word for it: He outshone Gutenberg as the sun outshines the moon!

Rumors began flying that Sir Isaac wasn't any easier to get along with than he had been on earth. Nevertheless, his outfit got results. Why not! They have access to authoritative answers on whatever baffled them on earth and a universe from which to requisition material! Then, however, they ran amok on how to use all this new knowledge and the technology it made possible. (I wouldn't want this to be noised around but I think that The Chief indulges them a bit too much. They are like kids with new toys and he lets them play!)

ANDY You better watch your mouth, brother! You were pretty close to taking the Holy Name in vain.

SIMONPETER Not so. You'd be surprised at how laid back everyone now is. Why, these top scientists run around in shorts, T-shirts and sandals called go-aheads. I would be ashamed for anyone to see my knobby knees! But I digress:

The computer network one of Newton's project groups invented and installed all over the place was THE CHIEF'S pride and joy. He awarded a solid platinum plaque to Newton and crew on the day it was turned on in 1777 CE, a mere 50 years after Sir Isaac Newton arrived! And guess which Section was to be the first beneficiary of his grand achievement? And whose idea was it? Matt and John who showed up one day, all excited about Newton's new invention:

"This one will blow your mind," Matt said. "I don't understand technology but computers are machines something like our minds. You can feed them any kind of information, they remember it and repeat it for you on demand. The network is just a whole bunch of computers connected together."

"The computer network makes this library obsolete," John added, pointing to old Johann Gutenberg's handiwork. "We've talked it over with The Chief and he agrees that it should be modernized. Once the Project is completed, Pete, you simply will enter a name into the computer and it will immediately tell you to admit the person to Heaven or direct him or her to The Other Side. Your Section's efficiency index will hit the roof!"

"You won't have to lift a finger, Pete." Matt said. "Newton's Task Force will deliver a turnkey job. And it will require a large team of experts to enter all of this information into the computer."

ANDY Sounds like the same song, second verse they sang when Gutenberg first modernized your library?

SIMONPETER Exactly the same. They adopted every technical advance before it was out of the box, so to speak, and made certain that THE CHIEF first heard about it from them. And I was not the only one who heard about revolutionary projects only after the implementation was underway. While Matt was still talking, construction crews began arriving and they went at their task with a will. They graded the site, knocked out walls and expanded our workspace to accommodate fifty or sixty workstations—each, a one-person room they called a cubbyhole. When they were finished, another team moved in and installed the computer equipment. It was the strangest machinery I had ever seen—a mirror-like device that showed text or pictures from inside, a flat slab about the size of a lute with letter and number buttons all over it and a black box that made all of it work when it was invisibly connected together.

ANDY I'm going to have company so keep talking or whatever you usually do. I'll call you again when I'm alone.

(Switch fromTTX)

Then a third team arrived and they were even stranger than the computer equipment. Lucky for me, their chief was a brilliant guy named Jacob—not our ancestor—who briefed me on exactly what they were going to do and, when they finished, how they were going to train my staff and me to operate efficiently.

"Don't worry," Jacob said, "If you can push the right button, we will have you processing applicants at a blistering pace! This is the greatest invention since the wheel and your Section is the first to have it. But first, we have to enter all the information from your library into the main computer that's located elsewhere. That's what the computer work stations are for: Each operator will enter the information by pushing buttons on this keyboard."

"Suppose," I asked, "that someone pushes the wrong button and later, I enter a name and send him or her off to the wrong place?"

For Heaven's Sake

"Good point," Jacob said. "We anticipated it by dividing this project team into three sub-teams—two input (IP) sub-teams and one quality control (QC) sub-team. Each IP sub-team works independently, inputs information from the same books and forwards it to the QC sub-team. It in turn compares the two inputs and the computer kicks out any discrepancies which the QC sub-team then analyzes and corrects to match the original information in your library books."

"What if the IP sub-teams make the same mistake?"

"Well," Jacob scratched his head, "statistically, it's unlikely but I have to admit it's possible. If it happens, it happens. Hopefully, any misfit will raise a ruckus and demand a review. It's really not my problem."

My staff and I processed very few applicants while this project was underway but eventually it was completed, we were trained and the project teams moved on to other tasks. It felt odd since only four of us were working in a huge room fully equipped to accommodate sixty-four workers.

Imagine how odd I felt a few earth days later when the e-mail from HUMAN RESOURCES (the new name of the old PERSONNEL SECTION) appeared in my inbox. At that moment, I became a SECTION of exactly ONE! Since that day of infamy I have been on my feet at The Gate without a real break for a little over 200 years. You already have the message that I called the last straw! Please listen to it.

(Switch to TTX.)

ANDY I heard it. My communicator has fast speak, so I caught up with you as soon as my visitor left. I'm beginning to get the picture, although I don't know what you expect JC to do about it. Seems to me, you can keep plugging away at processing new arrivals. Do what you can. The rest of it isn't your problem.
SIMONPETER That's easy for you to say, brother. But you aren't facing a horde of impatient applicants who make Emperor Titus look positively benign. You do remember what he did to Jerusalem? Suppose this horde in Limbo decides to

storm THE GATE? They wouldn't leave enough of me to sweep up!

And for your information, I didn't wait for 200 years without trying desperately to solve the problem without bothering anyone about it. Indeed, I thought it was solved when a man by the name of Morse arrived in 1872 CE.

Somehow, he made it to The Gate without delay and, unlike many approved applicants, was in no hurry to go in. "What," he demanded as he stared at my computer, "is that electrical contraption?"

"My computer," I answered politely.

"What does it do?" He persisted.

I hemmed and hawed a bit because I still have no clear idea of how it works although I am proficient at using it.

"Come on, sir. I'm technically qualified by my work on earth to understand electrical phenomena. You surely must know of my successful installation and operation of a telegraphic system between Washington and Baltimore. It appears to me that you have a roomful of electrical devices and I am greatly interested in what I see here."

He wouldn't take no for an answer so I invited him to sit down at our training station and he literally took the training course. In fact, he caught on quickly and was so proficient that I took a deep breath, overstepped my authority and suggested that he might like to volunteer as my assistant. I even hinted that helping out at the gate was one of the prestige volunteer activities in Heaven.

"Maybe later," Morse said. "First, I want to find out what other surprises are in store for me here. By the way, who invented this equipment?"

"Sir Isaac Newton and his Think Tank."

"Ah ha! And where will I find him and it?"

So I told him. Morse and I actually became good friends. He dropped by from time to time and helped me process applicants. He also told me why no one had bothered to pick up all the equipment the installation teams had left behind.

"It's all obsolete," he said. "First generation, horse and

buggy stuff. Haven't you seen the current models? If I were you, I'd requisition new terminals and demand an adequate staff. In fact, even artificially intelligent computers are already available here. With a bank of them, you could clear up the backlog waiting in Limbo. If it's ok with you, I'll see what can be done."

Later, he told me that he had tried without success to interest Sir Isaac's Think Tank and that was that. Now you know the rest of the story and why I want to transfer to another section. Please! Please! Talk it over with JC and get back to me asap. I'm desperate!

ANDY I'll give it a try, but don't get your hopes up!

From: "JC" <jchrst@etrnl.hvn>
To: "SIMONPETER" <sptr4/12gtkpr@etrnl.hvn>

Sent: wx39

Subject: Your Problems

Hi, Simon,

Good to hear about you after all these years. By the way, Andy doesn't understand that he sends you normal e-mails unless he is talking directly to you. Our communicators are voice/only devices and we have no keyboards or printers because they would be inappropriate here. But back to your problems.

Although I haven't had time to listen to the messages you sent Andy, he summarized them for me, explaining that you are having what sounds like a career crisis. As I understand it, you are feeling overworked and under-appreciated because of modernization and you believe that a career change is the only solution for your problem.

It's perfectly normal to feel fed up when things don't go exactly the way we want them to but frankly, I 'm disappointed that you want to abandon the assignment I gave you way back in what you seem to regard as the good old days. Of all my friends, Simon, you were the only one uniquely fitted to be The Gatekeeper.

Did I make a mistake? Have you given modernization a fair chance to prove itself? Have you explored all the alternatives? Have you looked deep inside yourself and made certain that your old headstrong demon hasn't followed you here? Have you considered what would happen to all of those people you claim are waiting in Limbo if you, the only experienced Gatekeeper in the Universe, called it quits?

Is modernization all bad? Remember that I said *works mightier than mine* would be done? Do you disapprove of medical science for eliminating some diseases and working

19

night and day to conquer others? If we could have flown from Galilee to Jerusalem, would you have preferred to slog it on foot down the Jordan valley or through the mountains of Samaria?

Are you disillusioned because Heaven is more like earth than you expected? Think about it, Simon. Sure, I sometimes get a little misty eyed for my home in Nazareth, even for the dung and dust of trails wide enough for a camel but too narrow for a cart. Everything was simpler and we had a lot of fun except for that run-in with the Sanhedrin and the Romans. Everyone seemed to have time to get to know each other although not many actually took the time to do it. The same old human perversity popped up then and keeps popping up now and even here.

Have you forgotten that life features both pleasures and one crisis after another? Have you any idea how many people on earth have starved to death or killed each other in feuds and wars or just for the hell of it since we went fishing in Galilee?

Next time you take a break, check on the Earth Mortality Tables for any century. The totals are staggering and one of my current assignments is trying to find a way to stop the slaughter short of killing the killers. And you know DAD, he won't hear of that. Says HE tried it once and it didn't work then and won't work now. So here I am, off in a corner of the Galaxy testing another proposed solution. From the way things are going, however, it may turn out to be a rerun of what happened on earth. I hope not because once was more than enough!

So Simon, I'm not now in a position to help with your transfer request. Indeed, I hope that you will reconsider your hasty decision. If you can arrange a short vacation, notify Andy in advance and come for a visit to Coordinates x2ly930z12. We would love to see you. –JC

From: "SIMONPETER" <sptr4/12gtkpr@etrnl.hvn>
To: "ANDY" <adrw6/12@etrnl.hvn>

Sent:wx66

Subject: My Problem's Solution

    I can't thank you enough for whatever you told JC that made him turn me down flat! His decision left me no choice and I have found a perfect solution to my problem. Well, I didn't exactly find the solution; it found me. It's so simple that I should have thought of it ages ago!

    As I told you, Limbo is swarming with millions of people waiting to learn whether or not Heaven is their destination. They're all mixed up; brand new arrivals have made it to the head of the pack while others have been sidelined for centuries. It's a real mess, although many of the new arrivals are computer literate and on earth, they cut their teeth on modernization. It never occurred to me that one of them might help solve my problem. But that is exactly what happened:

    Usually, everyone that I approve for entry into Heaven can't wait to go inside. In fact, some of them are quite upset about the time it takes to match a name to the records and to make sure that no errors occur. Occasionally, an approved applicant likes to chat a bit before going in and I always enjoy a break from the routine.

    That's how I met Rance who only has one name. Searching for his record took a long time because a single name in a list that usually features several names per individual poses special problems. While we were waiting for results, Rance motioned to the large number of unoccupied terminals in our work room and asked:

    "How's come you're the only one on duty?"

    "It's a long story and I won't bore you with details. The truth is, I'm THE Gatekeeper, the one-man Entrance Section on Heaven's Organization Chart! I've been on my feet without a real break for about 200 years and no one pays attention to my pleas for help!"

"You've got to be kidding! Are all of these computers in working order?"

"As far as I know, yes."

"Man, it's weird to let them sit there idle! But I have an idea. Can I bunk here for a while and do a little recruiting?"

"Few people want to postpone entry, but I guess it's ok. Anyway, work room is part of Heaven. What does recruiting mean?"

"Man, we're going to staff your Section with computer experts from Limbo. They have the most powerful of all reasons to volunteer: In exchange for their assistance, you promise to process them ahead of the mob. It's like a self-check-out market or self-check-in airport. On earth, getting customers to work for free was the hottest business idea of the 20th century!"

Rance's proposal was exciting and we began outlining the details: A volunteer would work 24 hours per day for 7 earth days—roughly equivalent to a month of work on earth at five 8-hour days per week. Heaven, of course, doesn't actually measure time in earth units but we used them so the volunteers would understand their limited commitment and that it absolutely would not affect their screening for Heaven or The Other Side.

At the end of the period, each volunteer would be required to recruit a replacement volunteer before his or her personal application could be processed. Only one hitch appeared:

"Rance, I doubt that a volunteer would wait 7 days to check his or her status. Maybe we ought to screen them and then only ask citizens of Heaven to volunteer."

"Good point. But once admitted to Heaven, what's the incentive for volunteering? Yeah, I know I did but I'm a nerd! Give me a few minutes on one of the computers and maybe I can come up with something."

He began fiddling with various buttons on the keyboard and brought up strings of what looked like meaningless symbols on the screen and said, "Ah ha! I can block a volunteer's name for as long as necessary. And even a skilled hacker can't unlock it without my key."

We then printed up a flyer describing the volunteer program and Rance disappeared out in Limbo. In less than half an hour, he returned with 75 to a 100 people, each waving a flyer and clamoring to volunteer.

Rance interviewed each of them, selected the number needed and, almost before you can say Jerusalem, the first Entrance Section volunteer staff assembled in the workroom for training. I merely stood around and tried to look busy while Rance did all the work. Suddenly, I realized that I had made a serious mistake: Since the Entrance Section workroom is part of Heaven, I had just admitted 60 unscreened applicants! Qualified or not, anyone of them could walk out the back door onto one of Heaven's streets.

I almost panicked! As nonchalantly as my quaking limbs would permit, I made my way to the back door, trying to remember if it was equipped with a lock, hoping that it was and that one of the keys on my ring would fit it. I also fervently hoped that Mama had been right in frequently saying that *"Heaven takes care of babes and fools"*!

She was! So I locked the door and then concealed it behind a large storage cabinet. No one noticed me because they were at the other end of the room, listening to Rance explain our operation. Silently, I vowed to permanently block the back door just as soon as this volunteer period ended.

Within a few hours, Rance had the volunteers trained and we began processing applicants at a fantastic rate. Now, I'm pleased to report, I am the CEO of the Entrance Section. We have a daily staff meeting and I have issued executive orders appointing Rance as Chief Operating Officer and Morse as Chief Technical Officer. (Morse had dropped by and was so impressed with our operational plan that he volunteered to serve as Chief Technical Officer!)

Everything is running so smoothly, it's almost too good to be true!—Simon

For Heaven's Sake

From: "JOHN" <jnz2/12hqhhmnrscrs@etrnl.hvn>;
"MATT" <mtthw1/12fnnc@etrnl.hvn>
To: "SIMONPETER" <sptr4/12gtkpr@etrnl.hvn>

Sent: wx74

Subject: Congratulations!

It gives us great pleasure to congratulate you on your outstanding performance during the previous reporting period.

Indeed, Simon, your efficiency index has literally hit the roof! It is such a spectacular increase over your previous performance that Matthew and I have assigned a team of efficiency experts to visit the Entrance Section and analyze exactly how you have achieved such superior performance. We are certain that you have some valuable secrets to share with your fellow Section Executives.

A special messenger soon will deliver an engraved *Outstanding Performance* plaque that you will be proud to display on your office wall!

A review of your Section's equipment also shows that you still have a first generation computer that should have been recycled ages ago. You should have requisitioned a new one when they were released. Nevertheless, using the obsolete computer makes your performance remarkable as well as outstanding!

A brand new computer is on the way to you and once you learn to operate it, your efficiency index undoubtedly will leave a trail of smoke! The installation team also will pick up the old equipment that was used during computerization of your library.

Keep up the good work! —John and Matt

From: "SIMONPETER" <sptr4/12gtkpr@etrnl.hvn>
To: "ANDY" <adrw6/12@etrnl.hvn>

Sent: wx74

Subject: FW "Congratulations"

Remember my e-mail that concluded with *Everything is running so smoothly, it's almost too good to be true?* Well, delete every word of that sentence except *it's too good to be true* and you will have an inkling of what is happening since I optimistically announced a solution to my problem.

Andy, I probably have set off a chain reaction by my successful and reasonable use of volunteers. I literally shudder to think of how John and Matt likely will react when they discover that they sent me the Outstanding Performance plaque based on their false assumption of how I achieved it. It's a beauty—a polished slab of jade with stars and the letters delicately engraved and then filled with gold. The stars are diamonds that direct your eyes to:

Outstanding Performance
SIMON PETER, THE GATEKEEPER

Ironically, they then dismantled the entire volunteer program before they even knew that it existed! Even so, the volunteers deserve high praise for their superior performance and as a tribute to them I intend to keep the plaque. Fortunately, it arrived just before the first volunteers were supposed to return to Limbo to recruit replacements. Talk about timing! If the e-mail from John and Matt had arrived three hours later, new volunteers would have been hard at work!

So I hurriedly called a staff meeting and we decided to process the entire volunteer staff without delay and to waive the requirement for recruiting replacements. I literally held my breath while Rance and Morse entered each name into the computer and the search began.

For Heaven's Sake

Although each volunteer had diligently fulfilled his or her commitment, I was certain that some of them would be disappointed and that I would be the bearer of the unwelcome news.

Directing applicants to The Other Side or welcoming them to Heaven respectively has always made me sad or joyful but no greater joy is possible than mine upon seeing opposite each volunteer's name on the screen the phrase *Approved for entry into Heaven*! We gave each volunteer a copy of the entire approved list and printed extra copies for the efficiency experts. I also informed the volunteers and my officers that I alone took responsibility for this operational experiment and that other officials of Heaven probably would want to question them about their volunteer work for the Entrance Section.

"I intend," I said, "to take full responsibility when the efficiency experts arrive to analyze our outstanding performance. Indeed, I am proud of what we have accomplished. If pressed, however, I will agree that future recruiting will be limited to pre-approved volunteers, provided sufficient new computers are installed or the obsolete ones remain in place. I would be pleased if each one of you would continue to work for the Entrance Section and I would appreciate suggestions for improving our efficiency and enhancing the volunteer experience."

Now I ask you, Andy: What else can I do? If you (or JC) have any suggestions, please get them to me without delay. I am prepared to grovel if that's what it takes.

--Simon

----Original Message----

From: "JOHN" <jnz2/12hqhhmnrscrs@etrnl.hvn> ; "MATT" < mtthw1/12fnnc@etrnl.hvn>
To: "SIMONPETER" <sptr4/12gtkpr@etrnl.hvn>
Sent :wx74
Subject: Congratulations!

----Original Message cont----

Odell Myers

It gives us great pleasure to congratulate you on your outstanding performance during the previous reporting period.

Indeed, Simon, your efficiency index has literally hit the roof! It is such a spectacular increase over your previous performance that Matthew and I have assigned a team of efficiency experts to visit the Entrance Section and analyze exactly how you have achieved such superior performance. We are certain that you have some valuable secrets to share with your fellow Section Executives.

A special messenger soon will deliver an engraved *Outstanding Performance* plaque that you will be proud to display on your office wall!

A review of your Section's equipment also shows that you still have a first generation computer that should have been recycled ages ago. You should have requisitioned a new one when they were released. Nevertheless, using the obsolete computer makes your performance remarkable as well as outstanding!

A brand new computer is on the way to you and once you learn to operate it, your efficiency index undoubtedly will leave a trail of smoke! The installation team also will pick up the old equipment that was used during computerization of your library.

Keep up the good work!—John and Matt

For Heaven's Sake

From: "MATT" <mtthw1/12fnnc@etrnl.hvn>
To: "SIMONPETER" <sptr4/12gtkpr@etrnl.hvn>
Cc:"JOHN"<jnz2/12hqhhmnrscrs@etrnl.hvn>;
"SECURITY"<scrty@etrnl.hvn>;"LEGAL" <lgl@etrnl.hvn>

Sent:wx73

Subject: Entrance Section Irregularities

My efficiency experts have given me a very disturbing report. Indeed, *disturbing* is much too mild a term for the reported breaches of trust, security, established procedures, budgetary constraints and just plain common sense. Whatever were you thinking about, Pete? Heaven encourages volunteering but the Organization Procedures Manual has very strict rules governing it. Recruiting volunteers in Limbo and actually rewarding them with most favored treatment actually violated both the letter and the spirit of those rules.

You have a lot of explaining to do: Admitting unscreened applicants into a workroom located in Heaven, allowing access to and temporarily blocking access to confidential records, ignoring staffing requirements, etc. Frankly, Pete, Heaven has never dealt with anything this serious and I certainly won't speculate on the outcome of the investigation. In your favor, of course, is your long record of service, the superior performance of the volunteers, your forthright description of exactly what happened and the list of volunteers involved. Each volunteer will be interviewed and representatives of the responsible Sections probably will interview you. Doubtless, all favorable facts will be carefully considered.

You should contact Legal and request the services of a lawyer before the investigation gathers momentum. Believe me, you'll need one!—Matt

"SIMONPETER"
"ANDY"

TTX: Deep Trouble/wx76spa

SIMONPETER My last e-mail and my last breath will soon coincide unless a miracle happens.

ANDY Always overreacting, aren't you. Now let me guess why you called: You're going to tell me something that I really don't need to know so please give me a break and make it brief.

SIMONPETER: Come on, Andy, I'm in deep trouble and I need help instead of *I told you so* because Matt says that I have broken every law on the books, most of which I never heard of! He claims that Heaven has never had to deal with a case as serious as mine.

ANDY So what can they do, expel you? Last I heard, once *in* means never *out*! You have it made for eternity. Matt knows this so he probably is scaring you on purpose.

SIMONPETER It's hard to figure out exactly what Matt thinks because he's all bent out of shape over sending me a commendation and having it blow up in his face. He urged me to get a lawyer before answering any more questions and I did. I now have a feisty lawyer from some place on earth called Washington, D. C.

ANDY What does he say?

SIMONPETER That my case is "unprecedented, serious but not hopeless. So far, the investigation is underway but no formal charges have been filed. None are likely to be filed until all of the interviews are completed and the delay gives us an opportunity to finesse the whole business: You admit no blame but simply resign and request another assignment. Everyone will be happy to let the matter drop. It's a classic solution, exactly like the way we handled sensitive personnel problems on earth. Just give the rascal a recommendation and a transfer to another department or company. Saved all kinds of trouble. So, Simon, what kind of career change appeals to you?"

ANDY Sounds more than a little devious but it might work.

For Heaven's Sake

Are you going to take your lawyer's advice?

SIMONPETER It's tempting and it might get me out of an impossible job at the Gate. But it seems disloyal to JC. If you were in my shoes, brother, what would you do?

ANDY Hold it right there, Simon. It's not my problem and I can't solve it for you. Just keep me informed and, if you actually resign, I'll try to smooth things over with JC. Sorry but he's expecting me so I have to run.—Andy

From: "SIMONPETER" <sptr4/12gtkpr@etrnl.hvn>
To: "ANDY" <adrw6/12@etrnl.hvn>

Sent: wx80

Subject: I'm off the Hook!

Right after our conversation, my lawyer showed up with the good news that no charges will be filed against me. He called the arrangement a *"consent decree"*. I signed a ream of papers admitting no guilt and received a folder full of Organization papers certifying that no harm had been done.

As part of the deal, I agreed to request reassignment. I am sending you a blind copy of my request so you can sort of prepare JC for news of what happened. I will send him a personal message later when I find out where I will be working.

I sure hope that he won't be angry with me.—Simon

From: "SIMONPETER" <sptr4/12gtkpr@etrnl.hvn>
To: "MANAGEMENT" <ORGmgmnt1=3@etrnl.hvn>
Bcc: "ANDY" <adrw6/12@etrnl.hvn>

Sent: wx80

Subject: Request for Reassignment

After honorably serving as Gatekeeper for almost two thousand earth years, I respectfully request reassignment to the Education & Entertainment Section.

My proven service records assure that the Education & Entertainment Section will benefit from my experience and capabilities and thus directly contribute to realizing the Section's objectives.

I am more than willing to share my experience with my replacement at the Entrance Section and to train him or her in effective gate-keeping procedures for a reasonable period of time. A period equivalent to approximately two earth weeks should be sufficient.

Therefore, I request reassignment concurrently with completion of the training and also request permission to take part of my accumulated vacation before actually reporting for duty. A vacation leave equal to an earth month will be sufficient for visiting JC and my brother Andy.

Simon Peter (also known as the Rock)—The Gatekeeper

Odell Myers

This is an automated intercept reply to subject request:
Personnel transfer requests must be submitted on *HQtsfr-6*
form.

To safeguard your privacy, the *HQtsfr-6* form is only
accessible at a secure site and it cannot be downloaded to your
computer. Therefore, you must work on-line, filling in the
information requested on the form.

Each item on this four-page form must be completed and
your immediate supervisor must sign the form using his or her
registered signature in the space provided on page 4.
Otherwise, your request will not be considered.

To access the form, merely click on *HQtsfr-6*. If you need
assistance in completing form *HQtsfr-6*, click the **HELP** button
in the upper right hand corner of form *HQtsfr-6* to find answers
to the FAQs and instructions for submitting unanswered
questions.

Have a nice day.

For Heaven's Sake

From: "SIMONPETER" <sptr4/12gtkpr@etrnl.hvn>
To: "JC" <jchrst@etrnl.hvn>

Sent: wx80

Subject: FW "Request for Reassignment"

Dear JC:
I have reconsidered my problem at the Gate as you
recommended in your e-mail. But it's no use pretending that
I'm doing a good job as Gatekeeper. I'm not and I know it!
So I have to ask for your help in reassigning me to another
Section. And I can't fill out a silly *HQtsfr-6* form without lying
through my teeth!
I'm truly sorry to fail you but I just can't cope with what has
happened since Heaven began importing earth-shaking ideas.
Modernization is the root of the problem. And *efficiency* has
become the magic watchword.
I am not a Luddite—some of them are still stalled at the Gate
and they described the shameful treatment they endured on
earth—but it's as plain as the nose on my face that *efficiency*
means inventing machines that perform the tasks once performed
by human beings; for example, machines that build houses
without carpenters, masons, plumbers, etc.
What happens to those workers replaced by the machines
and to the educated scientists and technicians who invented the
machines? What happens to the poor folks who never even
made it into the now surplus skilled work force? Until we
imagine and implement some revolutionary ideas, what has
already happened to Heaven's Entrance Section will keep
happening everywhere:
What happened at the Entrance Section?
The staff was progressively and mindlessly downsized until
only one human attendant remained on duty at the Gate! That's
me. I'm it! The entire staff!
Consequently, hordes of new arrivals have stalled in Limbo
and those clamoring to get through the Gate don't give me

enough time to sit down, let alone time to fill out a silly form that will wind up in someone's (excuse the expression) CYA file.

The backlog in Limbo is thicker than fleas on a dog and I actually have been on my feet without a real break for the last 200 (earth) years. Andy knows all about my valiant but futile efforts to solve the massive problems at the Gate with a team of volunteers so I won't bore you with further details. Suffice it to say that I am in deep trouble and resigning as Gatekeeper was the only honorable way out.

I sure miss the good old days when we were tramping around Galilee and occasionally dropping a net in the water for real fish. Your friend and faithful servant, SIMON PETER

----Original Message----

From:"HQHUMANRESOURCES" <hqhmnrsrcs@etrnl.hvn>
To: "SIMONPETER" <sptr4/12gtkpr@etrnl.hvn>

Sent: wx80

Subject: FW "Request for Reassignment"

This is an automated intercept reply to subject request: Personnel transfer requests must be submitted on *HQtsfr-6* form. To safeguard your privacy, the *HQtsfr-6* form is only accessible at a secure site and it cannot be downloaded to your computer. Therefore, you must work on-line, filling in the information requested on the form. Each item on this four-page form must be completed and your immediate supervisor must sign the form using his or her registered signature in the space provided on page 4. Otherwise, your request will not be considered.

----Original Message cont----

To access the form, merely click on *HQtsfr-6*. If you need

For Heaven's Sake

assistance in completing form *HQtsfr-6*, click the **HELP** button in the upper right hand corner of form *HQtsfr-6* to find answers to the FAQs and instructions for submitting unanswered questions. –Have a nice day.

Odell Myers

From: "JC" <jchrst@etrnl.hvn>
To: "SIMONPETER" <sptr4/12gtkpr@etrnl.hvn>

Sent: wx82

Subject: FW "Request for Reassignment" (Ref. only.)

Hi, Simon,

Good to hear from you again although I am disappointed that you are giving up on solving the problems at the Gate. Andy tells me that you really are in a tight spot. I wish that I could help work out a solution other that your resignation. But I can't abandon my work here. Not yet.

Here is Dad's personal e-mail address—"THE CHIEF" <*******@etrnl.hvn>. Only you will be able to use this address to contact Him because it has an unbreakable security lock that correlates with you as the sender.

One caution, however: Use it sparingly and keep your message brief. Just imagine the billions of requests that would swamp his inbox if everyone had his e-mail address!

If you can arrange a short vacation, notify me in advance and come for a visit to coordinates x2ly930z12. We—Andy and I—would love to see you.—JC

For Heaven's Sake

From: "SIMONPETER" <sptr4/12gtkpr@etrnl.hvn>
To: "THE CHIEF" <*******@etrnl.hvn>

Sent: wx83

Subject: My Resignation and Request for Reassignment

Dear CHIEF:

Only with JC's encouragement would I dare to send You this message but there's serious trouble at the Gate and I'm right smack dab in the middle of it.

When JC gave me the keys of the Kingdom back on earth, I felt so honored I almost burst with holy joy! I didn't then understand that the keys involved a permanent assignment. Even so, when I arrived here, I enthusiastically threw myself into Gatekeeping, never expecting things in Heaven to become like things on earth and that I might not be equal to the task. But I'm not.

Cross my heart and hope to…well, You know what I mean: I'm no longer up to the task. That's the real reason I requested a transfer to the Education & Entertainment Section and also the reason I can't fill out form *HQtsfr-6*. I carefully read all four pages of that form and I would have to lie through my teeth in order to get a transfer using it.

So please, dear CHIEF, accept my resignation as The Gatekeeper and transfer me to the Education & Entertainment Section if there is an opening or any other Section where I can get off my feet. Since I arrived about 2000 years ago, my work often required me to keep one foot in Heaven and my off-foot in Limbo but for the last 200 years, I rarely have had time to sit down. If I were still on earth, I honestly would say that my feet are killing me!

Yours respectfully and urgently.—Simon Peter (sometimes called the Rock)

Odell Myers

From: "THE CHIEF" <*******@etrnl.hvn>
To: "SIMONPETER" <sptr4/12gtkpr@etrnl.hvn>

Sent: wx86

Subject: Your Resignation and Request for Reassignment

Dear Rocky, are you by any chance related to Knute Rockne? Splendid fellow! He and Vince Lombardi are co-executives of our Sports Section and they have organized all kinds of events including an absolutely fabulous football club. Yes, I am a fan of our *CHOSEN* team, although Knute and Vince are still showing me the fine points of the game! Since the game didn't exist when JC and you were young, I don't suppose you're much of a football player. Too bad because the club always has openings for pro-quality players. If you are pro-quality in any other sport, I can get you a tryout.

Except for Sports Section opportunities, however, no personnel transfers or new hires can be approved at this time. Of course I could just overrule this ban and do whatever I choose, but I am sure you agree that micro-managing one's executive staff absolutely destroys morale. Perhaps you are overreacting to aggravation that's normal in any endeavor. After all, you haven't been in the job very long. And believe me, I know how that goes! After the creation, I almost burned out. Creation itself was easy: I just said *"BANG"* and there it was. I had in mind something smaller but the universe took off at the speed of light and has been expanding ever since. Reminds me of *kudzu* in the United States. They ought to turn that stuff into fuel.

Expansion was just for starters. I only had one day of rest before the troubles began: Something broke and had to be fixed. Something else ran wild and had to be corralled! This ran out of fuel; that exploded; the low places flooded; the high places dried out; the plains burned into deserts and the seas froze into ice caps. And magma spewed out all over the place! *"The devil is in the details"* although I never caught him at anything until he got cocky and set up that scene with Eve. The consequences of that fiasco still plague me along with a universe-wide maintenance load that increased exponentially without even counting the problems caused by mankind!

As incredible as it sounds, the universe is so intricately interconnected that actions not only have equal and opposite reactions but also unequal, parallel and opposite chains of reactions, most of them not obviously related or traceable to specific actions. Believe me, Rocky, it's been a whole lot easier since I said *"hands-off"* and just let the universe run until we figure out how to get a handle on it without blowing it to smithereens.

That's why I formed the think-tank headed by Sir Isaac Newton. He has the best minds earth ever produced searching for a safe way to miniaturize the universe and reduce the time needed to develop habitable planets. Just between you and me, Newton's crew horses around too much but it keeps them happy; for example, they unmercifully rode Erwin Schrodinger:

"Before you were born in 1887," they gloated, "we solved the measurement paradox of your famous cat!" Then, they collapsed in gales of laughter before they got serious and showed Shrodinger the Quantum Computer they already were using for my very special projects.

For heaven's sake, Rocky, maybe you too ought to lighten up. Knute is sending you two complimentary tickets to the next football game. Take the afternoon off. Turn the gate-keeping chores over to your assistants, invite a friend and enjoy the game.—CHIEF

Odell Myers

From: "SPRTS" <EXkr@etrnl.hvn>
To: "SIMONPETER" <sptr4/12gtkpr@etrnl.hvn>

Sent: wx87

Subject: Complimentary Tickets

Dear Rocky,

Here per THE CHIEF'S request are two complimentary tickets to the next football game in the stadium: 0z141596 and 0z141597. At the gate, simply enter these codes into the entrance terminal.

The game between our *CHOSEN* team and *THE OTHER SIDE* team promises to be a most exciting one. Rivalry between these two teams is at a fever pitch and *CHOSEN* is the favorite since we will be playing on our home turf with the stands full of loyal fans. We need every advantage we can get because *THE OTHER SIDE* is one tough team. They know the rules and a hundred ways to break them without getting caught. Their coach whom I had rather not mention by name also has an uncanny way of getting first choice of pro-quality players.

Unfortunately, THE CHIEF had to permanently ban The Other Side fans from attending games because of their absolutely disgraceful behavior at the one previous game where we tried to be hospitable. They literally trashed the stadium and Security had a real problem restoring order. Actually, they didn't restore it. They had to use fire hoses in order to subdue the rioters before they could haul them, kicking, biting and screaming, back to The Other Side. In the interests of fairness, however, the game will be televised and their fans will be able to root to their hearts content via a return audio link.

I would like to invite you and your companion to be my personal guests on the *CHOSEN* bench for this important game and at my place afterward for an almost certain victory celebration.

---Knute

For Heaven's Sake

P. S. THE CHIEF said that you and I might be related. So please bring with you a copy of your ancestor/descendant chart.

Odell Myers

From: "SIMONPETER" <sptr4/12gtkpr@etrnl.hvn>
To: "SPRTS" <EXkr@etrnl.hvn>
Cc: "THE CHIEF" <*******@etrnl.hvn>

Sent: wx87

Subject: Football Game Tickets

Thank you for the subject tickets you forwarded per THE CHIEF'S request. I regret that I cannot use them and I assume they are not valid for future games. Unfortunately, I have no assistants, so I can't just shut the Gate and take an afternoon off. If circumstances allow me to attend a game in the future, I will request another ticket. One will be sufficient because my career assignment has left me no time to nurture old friendships or to cultivate new ones.

Attending a game, however, sure sounds exciting. And just thinking about sitting on the *CHOSEN* bench with the team makes me light headed because I have been on my feet without a break for about two hundred earth years.

When a game actually begins, how will I know which team to root for? Please recommend or send me some books and videos on the game of football. There's a lot to learn and I'm eager to get started.

Wouldn't it be exciting if you and I turn out to be related! (THE CHIEF calls me *Rocky* because I am often known as the Rock.) When we meet, however, I can't bring the *ancestry/dependency chart* that you mentioned because I don't have one. I sure wish that I had asked Daddy and Mama and other relatives about our ancestors. By the time I got interested in my roots, it was too late. Now when I inquire, they say *who cares!*

Yours truly. Simon Peter (You can call me Rocky.)

For Heaven's Sake

From: "SIMONPETER" <<u>sptr4/12gtkpr@etrnl.hvn</u>>
To: "THE CHIEF" <<u>*******@etrnl.hvn</u>>

Sent: wx90

Subject: Request for a Temporary Assistant

I sure appreciated the nice e-mail from Mr. Rockne and the complimentary tickets to the football game even though I could not use them. Declining his invitation to sit on the *CHOSEN* bench with the team made my feet ache something fierce!

Since permanent personnel transfers cannot now be approved, obtaining help through one of the temporary employee services listed on the Net would help solve the problem. It would be very economical, say, to use a Temp for at least 3 out of 10 work sessions.

If budget constraints exist, the easy way to handle it is to begin charging a small processing fee at the Gate. Not for admittance, of course, but just to cover the actual Temp cost plus the organization's normal overhead. (Think of it as a legitimate charge similar to shipping and handling on mail order purchases.)

Don't worry about applicant ability to pay the processing fee. You would be surprised at what they bring with them— cosmetics, clothing, jewelry, precious stones, gold and silver nuggets and coins, provisions sufficient for several years, horses, camels, sheep, cattle, dogs, cats, canaries, exotic animals, a retinue of slaves, an honor guard, medieval and modern armor, swords, guns of every make and kind, flame throwers, rocket launchers, Model T Fords by the dozen and occasionally a Rolls Royce or a Bentley. One man even showed up in a 1929 Model J Duesenberg Murphy Boat Tail Speedster, *one of a kind*, he said. A lady who called herself an aviatrix arrived in a fully armed P-38! It's a "US AIR FORCE" fighter airplane, a sort of metal bird without feathers. The wings don't even flap but it sure can fly!

Frankly, I only know the names of the modern stuff but not how it works or what it's good for. It's beyond me what anyone expected to do with the stuff they brought with them. I have had to fence off a big storage area for things they can't take inside. Thankfully, I don't have to feed any live animals along with my other overwhelming responsibilities. Moreover, each one has a tale that is absolutely incredible! It's all I can do to be polite when conversation shifts to subjects like men walking on the moon or heart and kidney transplants and other even more outlandish superstitious beliefs.

But I digress. My point is that most of them are loaded so a processing fee won't be a problem. If a really destitute person makes it to the head of the line, we can waive the fee.

And don't forget: Not everyone who makes it to the Gate gets in. Not by a long shot, no sirree! I apply the Standards. (By the way, the Standards are badly in need of an update. It can wait, however, until we solve the staffing problem.)

So, what do You think of my proposal? I am so excited about it that I couldn't wait to get the financials together before sending it to You. Right now, I am going to contact two or three Temp agencies for quotes and I'll get back to You asap! (That means as soon as possible.) It's an acronym that illustrates the many quaint but useful phrases that I have picked up on the job. I've had to become something of a linguist and my ordinary speech now is loaded with remnants of Aramaic, Hebrew, Greek, Latin, Spanish, English, etc. Please add *languages* to updating the Standards.—Yours hopefully, Rocky

For Heaven's Sake

From: "JOHN" <jnz2/12hqhhmnrscrs@etrnl.hvn>
To: "SIMONPETER" <sptr4/12gtkpr@etrnl.hvn>

Sent: wx94

Subject: FW "Request for a Temporary Assistant"; FW "Football Game Tickets" (Ref. only.)

My, you have been busy!

THE CHIEF asked my opinion on your "Request for a Temporary Assistant" in which you proposed using temporary personnel. And all I can say is *"Pete, Pete! Why didn't you contact me first?"* It would have saved THE CHIEF'S time and your considerable embarrassment. Surely you know that a Level Two Security Clearance is required for the position of Gatekeeper Assistant. Finding a temporary employee with a clearance only one level from the top is as likely as finding a flamingo that can play football!

My response to the CHIEF, however, will merely cite the security requirements in order to minimize your embarrassment. Now to your request in "Football Game Tickets."

That the subject e-mails arrived almost simultaneously means that you are in luck or it's a miracle. (Still hard to tell them apart, isn't it!) You probably will be surprised that the Human Resources Section, not the Main Library, is sending the football books and videos you requested. However, there's a good reason for our involvement:

As you probably know, Knute and Vince have endeared themselves to everyone here by organizing an absolutely fabulous sports program. I too have become a football and hockey fan! With them as mentors, you will learn to love the games and something a lot more important. Vince was popular on earth not only for coaching a winning team (the Green Bay Packers) but also for emphasizing that the same principles for coaching a team apply to running all types of organizations. After meeting Knute and Vince and seeing a few football games, I prevailed on them to discuss those principles with one of my associates. We then published that interview in an inspirational and absolutely indispensable book entitled WINNING IS FOREVER.

In the book and videos, you will discover all you need to know about football and, more importantly, <u>how to run your own department!</u> Its three sections, *Winning on Offense, Winning on Defense* and *The Winning Team,* are priceless! I urge you to read and re-read *The Winning Team.*

Let me be frank, Pete, because we once were teammates on earth. Even then, you were pretty headstrong and often too quick to speak or act without thinking. Remember sinking when you tried to walk on water? Or slicing off the ear of that servant of the High Priest who tried to arrest JC? Or what you said to the servant girl who asked if you were a Galilean?

And now: Bypassing the proper departments? Writing e-mails directly to the CHIEF?

Pete, that's not teamwork. And I don't mind telling you that I felt hurt and really disappointed when I received THE CHIEF'S request and a copy of your proposal. So join the team, Pete. And keep your eye on the ball! Hope to see you soon at a game. Now there's teamwork. Once you see how it works, I know I can count on you to play your position with your head, heart, hands and feet!—JOHN

For Heaven's Sake

From: "MATT" <mtthw1/12fnnc@etrnl.hvn>
To: "SIMONPETER" <sptr4/12gtkpr@etrnl.hvn>
Cc: "ZACK" <zck@etrnl.hvn>

Sent: wx94

Subject: FW "Request for a Temporary Assistant." (Ref. only.)

I am writing this e-mail because I just received the subject e-mail from The Chief with his terse command: *Matt, please handle this.* So I'm handling it. Note that a copy is being forwarded to Zack, the head of Purchasing. He took time off to attend the football game between the *CHOSEN* and *THE OTHER SIDE.*

I'm sure that you remember Zack, the little guy who climbed up in the tree for a better look at JC? Well, he reports to me since Purchasing is part of my Finance Section. Zack takes a very dim view of being bypassed, so thank your lucky stars that he was out of the office when The Chief's e-mail arrived, requesting Purchasing input on your proposal.

So I'll just lay it out for you in plain language: Never again go out for quotes on anything from paper clips to new planets! That's Purchasing responsibility. Get in touch with Zack. He'll furnish the right forms and assistance in following the established procedures. I strongly urge you to read and memorize the instructions in the Organization Procedures Manual.

Enough said! John mentioned your interest in football. It's a good game but too violent for my taste. I prefer baseball. Maybe we can get together at one of the league games. –MATT

Odell Myers

From: "THE CHIEF" <*******@etrnl.hvn>
To: "SIMONPETER" <sptr4/12gtkpr@etrnl.hvn>

Sent: wx95

Subject: Your proposal etc.

    I'm sorry your proposal for hiring temporary help at The Gate didn't work out. Actually, it seemed like a good idea until John and Matt explained why it wasn't feasible. But I haven't forgotten your problem and relief is on the way in the form of two amazing devices especially designed for you by team members of Sir Isaac Newton's think tank. Sir Isaac grumbled a bit at diverting former Nobel Laureates from serious work to designing what he called a *silly toy*. But, he agreed after Mr. Einstein volunteered to head up the project. Einstein was all excited because he said it was a perfect opportunity to do something creative with gravity. So a special messenger will deliver to you a custom designed seating system that looks like something out of a Star Ship. It will allow you to take the weight off your feet and make you feel like you're floating on a cloud. The system's loaded with adjustable features and with massaging modules that subtly and continuously relieve your tension from the soles of your feet to the top of your head. System power is a non-radioactive, self-renewing device that requires no fuel or batteries.

    The messenger also will deliver a custom designed container for soaking your feet while you are suspended in the seating system. The designers absolutely went wild on this item: It's self-cleaning, self-replenishing and self-powered with automatic temperature control. Just slip your feet into the liquid. They will know they've died and gone to Heaven!

    Confidentially, Rocky, I was so impressed with these inventions that I ordered a duplicate set for myself! I hope you like the gifts. –THE CHIEF

For Heaven's Sake

From: "SIMONPETER" <sptr4/12gtkpr@etrnl.hvn>
To: "THE CHIEF" <*******@etrnl.hvn>

Sent: wy25

Subject: Custom-designed Seating System and Bucket

Thank you for your kind words concerning my recent proposal and for the subject gifts. They were delivered at the same time as the football book and video from John. I was as excited as a birthday-kid wondering which gift to open first! However, I first dived right into the book, *WINNING IS FOREVER*, because John and Matt came down on me pretty hard for bypassing their Sections when I proposed hiring temporary help at the Gate.

The book was pretty confusing until I actually played the video of a football game. Whew! Is it really a game? It looks like a fight to the death between gladiators in the Coliseum!

Eventually I got the hang of it and began to see how I could become a valuable team player. *Winning on Defense* is right on target for my career as Gatekeeper. I imagined myself as guard, tackle or center, blocking and tackling anyone who tried to break through my defense or make an end run at the Gate. Matter of fact, I psyched myself up to a fever pitch and decided to try out your gifts just to relax.

After setting the temperature of the foot container—it looks like an ordinary bucket except for the controls—I climbed into the seating system, adjusted it for a quick exit and slipped my feet into the soothing liquid. Never have I been more comfortable! I processed applicants at a record pace. Then I almost went to sleep until startled awake at the sight of a veritable phalanx of figures approaching the Gate.

They were Indians still dressed in *dhotis* and nothing else. They marched right through the mob crowding the Gate until they were first in line. The front ranks parted and a tiny little lady stepped forward and introduced herself:

"Young man," she said, "I'm Teresa. Step down off that

Odell Myers

contraption and move aside so my friends and I can enter."

"Ma'am," I answered courteously, "please wait while I check the record…. No problem. The green light means you can go right in."

"Come on, men," she said. And the phalanx started to surge forward.

"Not so fast," I ordered as I stood up, blocking the way. "You are cleared to enter. But your friends must be cleared one at a time."

"No deal. We all go in or we stand here until you get your superior down here to…."

Well, I interrupted her and pointed to THE CHIEF'S letter appointing me as The Gatekeeper and she said:

"He's superior, all right. Please politely inform Him that I…"

While she was talking, I caught a glimpse of a person attempting an end run past the Gate. Quickly, I estimated his speed and track, crouched and lunged to intercept him. I was attempting to make what the football book calls a *flying tackle*—I understand that it's illegal in a game but it seemed appropriate under the circumstances—and I actually was airborne before I saw him plainly: He was about six foot six and weighed at least 275 pounds of pure muscle.

Just before I hit him, I realized that my feet were wedged tight in the custom designed bucket. I was like a flying projectile right on target but I didn't even slow him down. He swatted me as though I was a fly. I hit the wall and went out like a light!

I don't know how long I was unconscious. When I finally began to come around, Teresa was bathing my face with cool water and checking me over for broken bones. "Just take it easy, she said. "You had quite a jolt but you'll be ok. And don't worry, we have everything under control."

And they did: Teresa and her band of near naked Indians saved the day: The Indians caught that would-be intruder and dragged him back outside the Gate. Then they bunched themselves together—cheek to jowl, shoulder-to-shoulder—

51

and blocked the Gate.

I was so grateful for what they had done that I probably exceeded my authority by making a deal with Teresa:

"Give me a list of your Indian friends and go on in," I said. "I'll check the list as soon as possible. If I come up with any rejections, promise to deliver them to me without delay."

"It's a deal," she agreed.

CHIEF, I hope You can see Your way clear to approving a new proposal: Please appoint Teresa as Co-Gatekeeper and assign her Indian friends to create a new Gatekeeper Section. If so, YOU will never hear another peep out of me. We will manage the Gate like a pro-quality team and clear up the backlog. Our motto will be: *Win for THE CHIEF!*

I hate to report that the custom-designed bucket has disappeared and that the custom designed seating system was smashed to smithereens in the melee at the Gate. Please do not replace them. With my feet locked in the bucket, I lost confidence in *Winning on Defense.*

Please don't get John and Matt in an uproar over my next proposal. I might not take their complaints like a good teammate because I now am feeling exactly like my name: — Rocky

Odell Myers

From: "JIM—ED & ENT" <jms3/12@etrnl.hvn>
To: "SIMONPETER" <sptr4/12gtkpr@etrnl.hvn>

Sent: wy27

Subject: Teresa & Indians

I keep thinking you will show up at one of the absolutely stupendous educational or entertainment events that my Section offers free of charge:

Drama from Euripides to Henry Miller and beyond! Want to know who Will Shakespeare really was? Chat with him backstage after a rousing performance of Julius Caesar!

Literature? Homer! Dostoevsky, Bacon, Steinbeck, old Anthony Trollope! And even Anonymous? Well, *he* and/or *she* are here en masse!

Poetry? King David, Omar Kayyam, Donne, Keats, The Brownings, Frost, Emily Dickinson, Shelley, Neruda, Yevteshenko, Longfellow....

And Music? You have to hear it to believe it! Magnificent Mozart with the orchestra that also plays the music of the spheres! And that's just for starters!

Oh, I almost forgot: THE CHIEF asked me to respond to your message concerning Teresa and the Indians. I don't blame you for wanting them in your Section. But no dice! I have had an open requisition for her ever since hearing about her work on earth. So thanks for expediting her entry at the Gate. She and her troop are booked solid forever!

By special courier, I'm sending you some complimentary universal tickets and a flyer on upcoming events. Please come and *reach* as Robert Browning so aptly put it: *"Ah, but man's reach should exceed his grasp, or what's a heaven for?"* —JIM

From: "MANAGEMENT" <ORGmgmnt1=3@etrnl.hvn>
To: "SIMONPETER" <sptr4/12gtkpr@etrnl.hvn>

Sent: wy47

Subject: Staff Appointment

We take great pleasure in announcing the appointment of Bartholomew to head the newly created Executive Wholeness Section that has been established to coordinate for top-ranking personnel the rich menu of perks and activities freely provided in recognition of their extraordinary service and sacrifice.

Bart's mission: *NO EXEC LEFT BEHIND!* So, Simon Peter, here's Bart with a personal message and a list of the gifts now on the way to you by special courier:

1. An engraved, diamond-studded ETRNL Card, good for reserved-seat or first-class admission to every conceivable activity—game, lecture, drama, symphony, ballet, chorus, amusement park, zoo, museum, park…. If a ticket's required, you're in! No standing in line. And get this: It's also a prepaid, sky's-the-limit debit card, good anywhere in the universe and at any cash station without requiring a PIN number. It simply reads your retina. Foolproof, fraud-proof and indestructible! If misplaced, it automatically sends its coordinates to Security and requests rapid retrieval!

2. A UNIVERSAL MEMBERSHIP CERTIFICATE in every Sports-, Bridge-, Literature-, Science-, Travel-, etc. Club-. You're already listed at the top of every roll! Need equipment? A professional coach? Mentor? Personal tour conductor? No problem: Everything needed comes with the membership!

3. A UNIVERSAL WHOLENESS CARE CARD. On earth, they'd call it universal health care—no-paperwork, cradle to (excuse the expression) grave, no-deductible, no co-pay, unlimited prescription/non-prescription drugs, etc. Who needs it? You do, Simon, because your new body requires exercise,

proper care, periodic checkups, preventive and, as necessary, corrective maintenance. Just walk in to any of our conveniently located Wholeness Centers or, if necessary, hit the Panic button that's located on the Card and a Wholeness Team will pick you up pronto!

4. TRANSPORTATION. We've got you going in ways we couldn't even imagine when we were slogging it on foot around Galilee with JC! Your personal TRANSPER that makes any earthly transport look like a kid's toy is on the way to you. But it's hot! And I do mean HOT! So first take the operator's instruction course. Otherwise, SIMON, you might wind up as an ornament on the front of a massive TRANSPUB. They, of course, follow fixed routes and are great for going places on the routes.

Tops, however, for the times you'd really rather leave the driving to us is TRANSLIMO! You won't believe it until you try it! Here's how it works: On the front of your ETERNL Card, you will find a small circle marked *Talk*. Just touch it firmly and speak, saying whatever comes to mind; for example: *Come get me, Here boy* or just plain *Here*. Almost before you catch your breath, a chauffeured TRANSLIMO will pull up and take you wherever you want to go locally. It also works locally in distant destinations although travel agents must arrange long distance travel. Try to call a TRANSLIMO in an area not covered? No problem: A courteous voice will help you. Remember our motto: *NO EXEC LEFT BEHIND!* It's literally true!

5. COMMUNICATIONS? Now here's an area that keeps the experts up nights. We could've interconnected everybody on a celestial party line and let it go at that. But Sir Isaac's communications experts said *NO* because voice telecommunications started out that way on earth and failed miserably for technical reasons as well as privacy and security considerations. So we took their advice and approved the continuously improving designs they keep hammering out by the light, so to speak, of midnight oil.

Without going into a lot of technology that I don't

For Heaven's Sake

understand, you now have almost unlimited access via a staggering range of terminal devices to a multi-layered voice and data communication network. It has what the experts call continuously and randomly programmed multi-functional *firewalls* that are impregnable and they control access to the various network layers. The Other Side thugs called hackers keep hacking away at the walls, so far without success. Keeps them busy, I suppose!

The special courier will deliver to you a PORTABLE PERSONAL TERMINAL (PPT) that provides instantaneous wireless audio, video and text access to every known network in the universe including earth's Internet! You won't even have to set it up: Just turn it on and surf to your heart's content. Download music and videos without worrying about copyrights.

Games? Choose and play your pick. Video conferencing so life-like you'll think you're in the same room. The PPT fits easily in your pocket or briefcase yet offers you a full-size virtual keyboard whenever you need it. But remember, the following conditions always apply to using the PPT. If you violate them, it will automatically shut down and you wouldn't want to go through the embarrassing SECURITY procedures to reactivate it!

Never use the PPT for normal business or correspondence on the etrnl.hvn network. It is designed to connect you with the other resources of the universe under your preprogrammed address and signature: "P.SIMON" psmn_48@ppt.spl. It's better than having a personal slave!

6. HABITATION. I saved the best until last and you will have to go to it because it cannot come to you Brace yourself for a literally lofty surprise: The penthouse suite atop JUDAH TOWER, one of thirteen 49-story condominium towers arranged symmetrically around THE WINNER'S CIRCLE, a beautiful park, lush with green lawns and perpetually blooming trees and flowers. The plantings are arranged to reveal the Star of David and the view from the terrace of your penthouse is absolutely spectacular.

Odell Myers

Each penthouse is reserved for one of us thirteen apostles so we will be neighbors. The special courier will hand you the keys and clear title documents to your penthouse and you can move in as soon as you like. You'll never have to lift a finger to vacuum or mop the floors, cook meals, do the laundry, change sheets or whatever! Everything is, so to speak, on the house!

Contact me anytime if you have questions. —"BART" <brt7/12whlns@etrnl.hvn>

For Heaven's Sake

From: HUMAN RESOURCES" <hqhmnrsrcs@etrnl.hvn>
To: "SIMONPETER" <sptr4/12gtkpr@etrnl.hvn>

Sent: wy70

Subject: Vacations

This e-mail is an automated status report on your use of the subject benefit provided for personnel of your classification. Your *accumulated* vacation amounts to 1932.5 units—an incredible number that indicates perpetual neglect of a benefit essential to your personal wellbeing and the satisfactory performance of your assigned duties.

This is appalling! Therefore, a yellow flag has been placed on your personnel record as a critical alert that means: 1. Your job performance will be thoroughly reviewed in the near future. 2. Your physical condition will be thoroughly evaluated. This is mandatory and you will hear from a Wholeness Center immediately if not sooner.

— Let a smile be your umbrella!

Odell Myers

From: "HQ FINANCE" <hqfnnc@etrnl.hvn>
To: "SIMONPETER" <sptr4/12gtkpr@etrnl.hvn>

Sent: wy72

!!!!!!RED ALERT! OVERRIDE WORK in PROGRESS!
ACKNOWLEDGE NOW!!!!!!

Subject: Financial Irregularities and Remedies

This E-MAIL is addressed individually to each Section
Executive because recent random audits of several Section
financials have revealed that some executives are sleeping at
the switch. or—Heaven forbid—cooking the books. Why don't
we just deal with the bad apples, if any?

Although it's well known that one bad apple spoils the
barrel, it would be ineffective because the observed
irregularities are wide spread and indicate that Heaven's
Organizational integrity is at stake. Therefore, the following
actions and requirements are effective immediately:

1. While you are reading this, a Certified Forensic Audit
(CFA) team is already at your door to subpoena your financial
records and shredders.

2. All Section funds except those of Headquarters Finance
(HQF) have been frozen. You can continue to operate but each
expenditure request must be submitted to HQF and, if
approved, paid by HQF. Once the CFA has been completed and
independent operation has been authorized to resume, the
amounts paid by HQF on your behalf will be debited from your
frozen funds before the balance is again accessible to your
Section.

3. Immediately prepare a new zero-based budget for your
Section for the next period and immediately submit the budget
in triplicate to HQF. Contact HQF for guidance in preparing a
zero-based budget. —-Have a nice day.

For Heaven's Sake

From: "Dr.LUKE" <drlk@etrnl.hvn>
To: "SIMONPETER" <sptr4/12gtkpr@etrnl.hvn>

Sent: wy78

Subject: Mandatory Physical Evaluation

That yellow flag on your personnel folder literally set off the sirens in my Wholeness Center. Normally, this means a rescue unit arrives at your door without warning, picks you up and bodily delivers you to the Center for the most thorough physical examination in the universe.

But I turned off the siren. "I'll handle this one personally," I told my staff. "Simon's an old friend and there has to be a good reason why he hasn't had a physical since he arrived."

So here I am, old friend, the same Dr. Luke who used to run around with your—excuse the expression—nemesis, Paul. Happily, bygones really are bygones!

You will probably be amazed at our current high level of medical care. If on earth I had known what I know now, honesty would have compelled me to turn myself in for ignorance and possible malpractice! One thing I have learned here is that these new bodies of ours are very resilient and durable. Occasionally, they need tweaking a bit here or there but we've never lost a patient—a record that makes us proud.

So I want you to take it easy before you come in for your appointment at the Center early on wy80. Don't eat breakfast or drink anything except water. I personally will conduct your examination and in short order, I'll have you tuned up and running in tiptop form. When you return to work, your efficiency index will soar!

Your tests will be extensive, so plan on spending 3 earth days at the Center.—Dr. Luke

Odell Myers

From: "SIMONPETER" <sptr4/12gtkpr@etrnl.hvn>
To: "MANAGEMENT" <ORGmgmnt1=3@etrnl.hvn>
Cc: "THECHIEF"<*******@etrnl.hvn>;
"JC" <jchrst@etrnl.hvn>;
"MATT" <mtthw1/12fnnc@etrnl.hvn>;
"JOHN" <jnz2/12hqhhmnrscrs@etrnl.hvn>;
"JIMED&ENT"<jms3/12@etrnl.hvn>;"BART"
<brt7/12whlns@etrnl.hvn>;
"DRLUKE"<drlk@etrnl.hvn>;"HQFINANCE"
<hqfnc@etrnl.hvn>;
"HQ HUMANRESOURCES" <hqhmnrsrcs@etrnl.hvn>

Sent: wy80

Subject: FW "Staff Appointment"; FW "Vacations"; FW "Financial Irregularities and Remedies"; FW "Mandatory Physical Examination"

Well, I'm stunned! Overwhelmed! Perplexed! I don't know what to say, much less how to begin! So I just have to flounder on and hope that I don't make a complete ass of myself. From where I stand here at the Gate, ass-status seems to have enough room for me and others.

The Wholeness Perks are simply amazing and my ignorance just has to show itself in plain sight: For example, what in heaven's name is a *penthouse?* The only tower I ever heard of was Babel where the mishmash of languages occurred. (With all due respect, quashing that project was a big mistake. At the Gate, half my time is wasted just trying to figure out what language an applicant is speaking and then trying to find an interpreter in the crowd. If I find one, I stand there like a fool, wondering if he or she is convincing me to admit B's first cousin!)

Except for Bart's technical talk about communications, I think I understand what the other perks are for although I don't pretend to know how anything actually works. Especially, the TRANSPER! How did you know that red is my favorite color?

61

For Heaven's Sake

The courier parked it just inside the Gate where I can keep an eye on it. He said not to worry because it's programmed only for me and also has an alarm system loud enough to, excuse the expression, wake the dead!

I sure hope I get some time off in the near future so I can go for what's called a *spin*. Does that mean it will make me dizzy? I hope not because I got real dizzy once when I sneaked a ride in a Roman chariot. I was just a little guy and watching those wheels go round was too much. After that, I stuck to my own two feet and, occasionally, rode a four-footed ass. Maybe someday I'll understand what makes the TRANSPER go!

Meanwhile, please look at the forwarded e-mails. Reading them sequentially would stun a stone statue and should help *"MANAGEMENT"* understand why I am perplexed. Actually, I feel like I'm stuck at the bottom of Jacob's Well, looking up toward a small circle of light and asking *Is anyone there?* So far, all I've heard is an echo. Once, I even had a sort of waking dream that an ass's head appeared in the circle of light and on the off chance that he might have been a relative of Balaam's ass, I tried talking to him. He just shook his head and dislodged a rock that threatened to take my head off. Luckily, it was a dreamed-up rock!

According to *"Staff Appointment"*, I have been awarded an incredible number of benefits that I would dearly love to accept with my whole heart. For more than 200 earth years, however, I've stood on my feet in a dead-end job at The Gate. I am THE ONE & ONLY GATEKEEPER—the entire Entrance Section comprises exactly ONE MAN! ME! I'm it!

So how, for heaven's sake, can I move into my penthouse, enjoy the memberships, travel and entertainment, spend myself silly with the magic card and tryout my little red TRANSPER?

And no sooner had I got my hopes up that relief was on the way, the last three of the forwarded e-mails practically jumped off the screen into my lap:

"Vacations" chastised me for not taking a vacation, threatened me with a poor performance review and scared the living daylights out of me by hinting that I might not be well.

Odell Myers

I would dearly love to take a vacation and will do so when my previous requests for reassignment or assistants are approved. I also will welcome a performance review if the reviewer is at least able to distinguish between a single individual and a Section.

"Financial Irregularities and Remedies" froze my non-existent Section funds and the forensic CPAs complained because they could not confiscate non-existent financial records. They muttered that I had *"shredded the records"* and promised me a swift *"hearing from the authorities"*. I will surrender peaceably and agree to be held without bail to face the charges of shredding non-existent financial records. Please caution the arresting authorities to notify The Chief before removing me from my post and leaving the Gate un-staffed. As to the Finance Section order requiring a zero-based budget, I respectfully state that my Section is unfunded. *"Mandatory Physical Examination"* seems to be my best hope, thanks to my old friend, Dr. Luke. Unless he makes house calls, I request permission to close the Gate in order to go to the Wholeness Center for a long overdue physical evaluation. To tell the truth, I *may not be firing on all cylinders and I definitely need a tune up.* (These are expressions I picked up from the man who brought his Duesenberg with him.) If Dr. Luke has a good Podiatrist on staff, maybe he can do something to relieve my aching feet. –Hopefully, Simon Peter

----Original Message 1----

From: "MANAGEMENT" <ORGmgmnt1=3@etrnl.hvn>
To: "SIMONPETER" <sptr4/12gtkpr@etrnl.hvn>
Sent: wy47

Subject: Staff Appointment

----Original Message 1 cont----

We take great pleasure in announcing the appointment of

63

Bartholomew to head the newly created Executive Wholeness Section that has been established to coordinate for top-ranking personnel the rich menu of perks and activities freely provided in recognition of their extraordinary service and sacrifice.

Bart's mission: *NO EXEC LEFT BEHIND!* So, Simon Peter, here's Bart with a personal message and a list of the gifts now on the way to you by special courier:

1. An engraved, diamond-studded ETRNL Card, good for reserved-seat or first-class admission to every conceivable activity—game, lecture, drama, symphony, ballet, chorus, amusement park, zoo, museum, park…. If a ticket's required, you're in! No standing in line. And get this: It's also a prepaid, sky's-the-limit debit card, good anywhere in the universe and at any cash station without requiring a PIN number. It simply reads your retina. Foolproof, fraud-proof and indestructible! If misplaced, it automatically sends its coordinates to Security and requests rapid retrieval!

2. A UNIVERSAL MEMBERSHIP CERTIFICATE in every Sports-, Bridge-, Literature-, Science-, Travel-, etc.-Club. You're already listed at the top of every roll! Need equipment? A professional coach? Mentor? Personal tour conductor? No problem: Everything needed comes with the membership!

3. A UNIVERSAL WHOLENESS CARE CARD. On earth, they'd call it universal health care—no-paperwork, cradle to (excuse the expression) grave, no-deductible, no co-pay, unlimited prescription/non-prescription drugs, etc. Who needs it? You do, Simon, because your new body requires exercise, proper care, periodic checkups, preventive and, as necessary, corrective maintenance. Just walk in to any of our conveniently located Wholeness Centers or, if necessary, hit the Panic button that's located on the Card and a Wholeness Team will pick you up pronto!

4. TRANSPORTATION. We've got you going in ways we couldn't even imagine when we were slogging it on foot around Galilee with JC! Your personal TRANSPER that makes any earthly transport look like a kid's toy is on the way to you. But it's hot! And I do mean HOT! So first take the operator's

instruction course. Otherwise, SIMON, you might wind up as an ornament on the front of a massive TRANSPUB. They, of course, follow fixed routes and are great for going places on the routes.

Tops, however, for the times you'd really rather leave the driving to us is TRANSLIMO! You won't believe it until you try it! Here's how it works: On the front of your ETERNL Card, you will find a small circle marked *Talk*. Just touch it firmly and speak, saying whatever comes to mind; for example: *Come get me, Here boy* or just plain *Here*. Almost before you catch your breath, a chauffeured TRANSLIMO will pull up and take you wherever you want to go locally. It also works locally in distant destinations although travel agents must arrange long distance travel. Try to call a TRANSLIMO in an area not covered? No problem: A courteous voice will help you. Remember our motto: *NO EXEC LEFT BEHIND!* It's literally true!

5. COMMUNICATIONS? Now here's an area that keeps the experts up nights. We could've interconnected everybody on a celestial party line and let it go at that. But Sir Isaac's communications experts said *NO* because voice telecommunications started out that way on earth and failed miserably for technical reasons as well as privacy and security considerations. So we took their advice and approved the continuously improving designs they keep hammering out by the light, so to speak, of midnight oil.

----Original Message 1 cont----

Without going into a lot of technology that I don't understand, you now have almost unlimited access via a staggering range of terminal devices to a multi-layered voice and data communication network. It has what the experts call continuously and randomly programmed multi-functional *firewalls* that are impregnable and they control access to the various network layers. The Other Side thugs called hackers keep hacking away at the walls, so far without success. Keeps them busy, I suppose!

The special courier will deliver to you a PORTABLE PERSONAL TERMINAL (PPT) that provides instantaneous wireless audio, video and text access to every known network in the universe including earth's Internet! You won't even have to set it up: Just turn it on and surf to your heart's content. Download music and videos without worrying about copyrights.

Games? Choose and play your pick. Video conferencing so life-like you'll think you're in the same room. The PPT fits easily in your pocket or briefcase yet offers you a full-size virtual keyboard whenever you need it. But remember, the following conditions always apply to using the PPT. If you violate them, it will automatically shut down and you wouldn't want to go through the embarrassing SECURITY procedures to reactivate it!

Never use the PPT for normal business or correspondence on the etrnl.hvn network. It is designed to connect you with the other resources of the universe under your preprogrammed address and signature: "P.SIMON" psmn_48@ppt.spl. It's better than having a personal slave!

6. HABITATION. I saved the best until last and you will have to go to it because it cannot come to you Brace yourself for a literally lofty surprise: The penthouse suite atop JUDAH TOWER, one of thirteen 49-story condominium towers arranged symmetrically around THE WINNER'S CIRCLE, a beautiful park, lush with green lawns and perpetually blooming trees and flowers. The plantings are arranged to reveal the Star of David and the view from the terrace of your penthouse is absolutely spectacular.

Each penthouse is reserved for one of us thirteen apostles so we will be neighbors. The special courier will hand you the keys and clear title documents to your penthouse and you can move in as soon as you like. You'll never have to lift a finger to vacuum or mop the floors, cook meals, do the laundry, change sheets or whatever! Everything is, so to speak, on the house!

Odell Myers
Contact me anytime if you have questions.—"BART"
<brt7/12whlns@etrnl.hvn>

----Original Message 2----

From:"HQHUMANRESOURCES" <hqhmnrsrcs@etrnl.hvn>
To: "SIMONPETER" <sptr4/12gtkpr@etrnl.hvn>

Sent:wy70

Subject: Vacations

This e-mail is an automated status report on your use of the subject benefit provided for personnel of your classification. Your *accumulated* vacation amounts to 1932.5 units—an incredible number that indicates perpetual neglect of a benefit essential to your personal wellbeing and the satisfactory performance of your assigned duties.

This is appalling! Therefore, a yellow flag has been placed on your personnel record as a critical alert that means: 1. Your job performance will be thoroughly reviewed in the near future.

2. Your physical condition will be thoroughly evaluated. This is mandatory and you will hear from a Wholeness Center immediately.

Let a smile be your umbrella.

----Original Message 3----

From: "HQ FINANCE" <hqfnnc@etrnl.hvn>
To: "SIMONPETER"<sptr4/12gtkpr@etrnl.hvn>

Sent: wy72
!!!!!!RED ALERT! OVERRIDE WORK in PROGRESS!
ACKNOWLEDGE NOW!!!!!!

Subject: Financial Irregularities and Remedies

    This E-MAIL is addressed individually to each Section Executive because recent random audits of several Section financials have revealed that some executives are sleeping at the switch or—heaven forbid—cooking the books. Why don't we just deal with the bad apples, if any?

    Although it's well known that one bad apple spoils the barrel, it would be ineffective because the observed irregularities are too wide spread. They constitute a pattern and indicate that Heaven's Organizational integrity is at stake. Therefore, the following actions and requirements are effective immediately:

    1. While you are reading this, a Certified Forensic Audit (CFA) team is already at your door to subpoena your financial records and shredders.

    2. All Section funds except those of Headquarters Finance (HQF) have been frozen. You can continue to operate but each expenditure request must be submitted to HQF and, if approved, paid by HQF. Once the CFA has been completed and independent operation has been authorized to resume, the amounts paid by HQF on your behalf will be debited from your frozen funds before the balance is again accessible to your Section.

    3. Immediately prepare a new zero-based budget for your Section for the next period and immediately submit the budget in triplicate to HQF. Contact HQF for guidance in preparing a zero-based budget.—Have a nice day.

Odell Myers
----Original Message 4----

From: "Dr.LUKE" <drlk@etrnl.hvn>
To: "SIMONPETER"<sptr4/12gtkpr@etrnl.hvn>

Sent:wy78

Subject: Mandatory Physical Evaluation

That yellow flag on your personnel folder literally set off the sirens in my Wholeness Center. Normally, this means a rescue unit arrives at your door without warning, picks you up and bodily delivers you to the Center for the most thorough physical examination in the universe.

But I turned off the siren. "I'll handle this one personally," I told my staff. "Simon's an old friend and there has to be a good reason why he hasn't had a physical since he arrived."

So here I am, old friend, the same Dr.Luke who used to run around with your—excuse the expression—nemesis, Paul. Happily, bygones really are bygones!

You will probably be amazed at our current high level of medical care. If on earth I had known what I know now, honesty would have compelled me to turn myself in for ignorance and possible malpractice! One thing I have learned here is that these new bodies of ours are very resilient and durable. Occasionally, they need tweaking a bit here or there but we've never lost a patient—a record that makes us proud.

So I want you to take it easy before you come in for your appointment at the Center early on wy80. Don't eat breakfast or drink anything except water. I personally will conduct your examination and in short order, I'll have you tuned up and running in tiptop form. When you return to work, your efficiency index will soar!

Your tests will be extensive, so plan on spending 3 earth days at the Center.—Dr. Luke

For Heaven's Sake

From: "PAUL" <pl13/12@etrnl.hvn>
To: "SIMONPETER" <sptr4/12gtkpr@etrnl.hvn>

Sent: wy82

Subject: Debater's Club

As chairman of the Debater's Club, an independent entity not affiliated with or controlled by any Section, I am pleased to extend to you an almost unanimous invitation to join the club. Don't let the *almost unanimous* phrase discourage you because the moment we reach a unanimous decision on anything, the Debater's Club will dissolve and disappear.

I look forward to continuing our debates because you always said *However* to *Whatever* idea of mine that clinched the debate in my favor. Perhaps here, you will not be so hard-headed.

The Club membership includes a galaxy of stars and, excuse the expression, a few black holes whose qualifications leave much to be desired. Nevertheless, the roster reads like the who's who of the ages—Moses, Job (Surprise! Turns out he really is real!), Jewish prophets by the dozen, Aristotle, Plato, Augustine, Aquinas, Mohammed, Luther, Erasmus, Calvin, Knox, the Wesleys, Campbells, Abraham Lincoln, Stephen Douglas, Joseph Smith, Locke, Kierkegard, Kant, Nietzsche, the Niebuhrs, Otto, W.E.B. Du Bois, Martin Luther King Jr., Popes by the score (they especially urge you to join), Dalai Lamas, Buddha, etc.

You will be amazed to hear what's made of the Good News, the one point on which you would expect everyone here to finally agree. The dues are modest, just enough to cover printing an occasional program and serving refreshments after each meeting. Then, I'm sad to report, a few members always refuse to attend because of a too-heated exchange during the session.

I'm looking forward to seeing you and introducing you to the membership. –Paul

Odell Myers

From: "SIMONPETER" <sptr4/12gtkpr@etrnl.hvn>
To: "PAUL" <pl13/12@etrnl.hvn>

Sent: wy82

Subject: FW "Debater's Club" (Ref. only.)

Thanks, I think, for the invitation to join the Debater's Club. Sounds like you have found your niche because you undoubtedly are the most argumentative man I ever met. I hope that all of your debates occur on the ground floor because I seem to remember hearing of an incident in Troas where you droned on and on and literally bored the life out of a young man who went to sleep and fell out of a third-story window!

As to our earthly debates, I can't recall losing a single one! Oh well, old friend, I still miss those times on earth and I have mellowed.

I wish that I could accept your invitation but it isn't possible, at least not yet. Would you believe that I have been on duty here at the Gate ever since I arrived? And thanks to a juggernaut called *modernization*, I currently am the entire Entrance Section! Yes, a one-man Section, thanks mainly to Matthew and John.

My objective right now is obtaining help or reassignment to other duties. So far, my pleas have met with a formidable array of rejections. Instead of living beings, one of those computers appears to be answering a lot of my e-mails. If my hunch is right, I may be stuck at the Gate forever.

Had a nice note recently from your friend, Dr. Luke. I am hoping that he can examine me and put me on sick leave. My feet alone are physically unfit for Gate-keeping. If it's ok, I'll take a rain check on your invitation.—Simon

From: "SIMONPETER" <sptr4/12gtkpr@etrnl.hvn>
To: "MAINTENANCE" <mntnc@etrnl.hvn>

Sent: wy83

Subject: Gate Repairs & Minor Addition

A recent action by unruly applicants at the Gate damaged one interior wall that must be repaired. Narrowing the entrance space to accommodate one applicant at a time also has become necessary to avoid similar riotous incidents in the future. A rough sketch of the addition is available to guide the craft persons. Since the addition will occupy open space, no structural changes to the wall are required. Therefore, no permit is necessary and costs will be well within my maintenance budget. Please have a competent craft person contact me at the Gate asap.

S. Peter, Gatekeeper

From: "MATT" <mtthw1/12fnnc@etrnl.hvn>

To: "SIMONPETER" <sptr4/12gtkpr@etrnl.hvn>

Sent: wy83

Subject: FW "Gate Repairs & Minor Addition" (Ref. only.)

Not again, Pete! Using maintenance funds for capital improvements is strictly forbidden. I'm surprised that you again bypassed proper channels by dubbing the project a *minor addition.* Moreover, your Section is operating without approved capital or maintenance funds since you refused to resubmit a zero-based budget. Action is pending on this rather childish outburst.

I'd sure hate to see you traded after all we went through together on earth but a winning team is not made up of solo players. Better think about it, Pete. If you wait too long, it will be impossible to avoid the consequences. —MATT

For Heaven's Sake

From: "P. SIMON" <psm_48@ppt.spl>
To: "HQ" <cnstrtn&rpr@tmprl.lmb>

Sent: wy84

Subject: Addition at THE GATE

Have noticed your pop-up advertisements and request that a
representative contact me at the Gate asap in regard to subject
addition. A rough sketch of a small, freestanding structure that
will narrow the entrance for one-at-a-time service will be
available for inspection.

Structure envisioned is essentially a vertical cylinder having
one open, wedge-shaped compartment sized for only one
person. Cylinder must revolve under Gatekeeper control and
completely block the Gate until Gatekeeper decides otherwise.
An applicant simply steps into compartment, Gatekeeper
rotates cylinder until applicant appears at examination window.
Then, cylinder may be rotated in one direction to allow entry or
in opposite direction to deny entry.

Structure including examination booth to be constructed of
metal and very strong glass or transparent plastic. Therefore,
your representative must be technically competent with these
materials. Structure must not attach to or in any way modify the
Gate or the Wall. Coordination with other Sections not
authorized or required.—P. SIMON

Odell Myers

From: "HQ" <cnstrtn&rpr@tmprl.lmb>
To: "P. SIMON" <psm_48@ppt.spl>

Sent: wy86

Subject: Gate Addition

Every client ought to specify requirements as clearly as you did for the subject addition at the Gate. You made my job easy.

Don't worry about required payment in US dollars. (See your copy of the contract.) Just transfer the coin of the realm, so to speak, at the current exchange rate—1/3rd now, 1/3rd at delivery, 1/3rd at completion.

You'll save a bundle because you actually specified a revolving door like those installed in public buildings in major US cities. Chicago has hundreds of them.

And confidentially, our firm has hundreds of connections in Chicago! We can obtain the door assembly and mount it with the examination booth on a portable platform and the whole shebang will be in place almost before you can say Jerusalem.

Afterward, be my guest at the happy hour and, if we aren't too happy, at dinner!

—Annie

Architect, Construction & Repair, Ltd.

For Heaven's Sake

From: "P. SIMON" <psm_48@ppt.spl>
To: "HQ" <cnstrtn&rpr@tmprl.lmb>

Sent: wy96

Subject: Addition at THE GATE

Attn: Annie, Architect

   If my feet weren't still sore, I would dance with joy at the success of the subject addition. I can't imagine how they use revolving doors in Chicago but their performance here exceeds my wildest dreams! It is—excuse the expression—pure heaven! And the executive swivel chair with adjustable back and armrests is really a nice touch! My whole body is very grateful!
   I've been processing applicants at an astounding rate since I don't have to worry about sneaky end runs!
   Despite my total satisfaction with the project, I don't think it would be a good idea to feature me in a "satisfied customer" advertisement as you suggested. My Management frowns on that sort of publicity and besides, the Legal Section would make a federal case out of it before issuing a negative ruling.
   I also regret that a previous engagement prevented my joining you for the happy hour and dinner. I'm not exactly sure what a happy hour is but it sure sounded like fun.—P. SIMON

From: "B" <BlzB@othrsd.prm>
To: "P. SIMON" <psm_48@ppt.spl>

Sent: wz10

Subject: The Gate Project

Well hello again, Simon. Couldn't help but notice your private network address and almost failed to recognize you. The last time we met, I thought that you would be playing on my team. But what the hell—excuse the expression—*You can't win 'em all,* I always say. *C'est la guerre, etc., etc.,* and no hard feelings. So let's get down to business on your little secret project. My, you are a sly one, SI. You don't mind if I call you SI? Thought not.

How did you like Annie, my architect? I'll bet she rattled your old—excuse me—*new* Jewish cage! I almost hate to send her out on assignments. Sometimes she's gone for days. Know what I mean! I just loved this line in your e-mail to Annie: *I regret that a previous engagement prevented my joining you etc., etc.* Got cold feet, didn't you! Shame on you, SI!

Now what's all this about not knowing that Construction & Repair Ltd. is one of my subsidiaries? And why are you whining about the bill for removing your little secret project? Didn't you read the company profile on its home page? Is it my fault that an overweight lady got stuck in the revolving door? Did I force you to call Construction & Repair Ltd? Didn't you authorize the crew to transport the whole shebang to the company shop in order to free her? Why didn't you call *you know who*? *Why* indeed!

SI, you aren't exactly in a favorable bargaining position but far be it from me to take advantage of you. The whole shebang now isn't worth a plugged nickel because we had to cut it apart. It's not even worth scrap! And the labor took a lot of extra time to avoid hurting the fat lady. By the way, I pay my crews a lot more than Union scale.

I'm fair-minded, so here's the deal: $20,000 US, cash on the barrelhead. That's the best I can do. I won't make a red cent. In fact, 20K won't even cover my costs. Just transfer the payment to Construction & Repair Ltd. If you're strapped for cash, one of my other subsidiaries can arrange a personal loan.

Unless you prefer to deal with your own credit union! (Ha! Ha!) And we'll never mention your e-mails inviting Construction & Repair Ltd. to handle your little secret project or telling Annie how much you liked it. How did you put it? Oh, I remember: *"It's—excuse the expression—pure heaven!"* SI! SI! You're—excuse the expression— killing me!

Oh, I almost forgot: The bill is payable on demand and this e-mail is *the demand*. So I know you'll want to take care of it right away.—**"B"**

P.S. Annie sends her regards and says that she will be glad to design a foolproof replacement for the failed project. SI, you rascal! I do believe she's taken a shine to you!

Odell Myers

From: "SIMONPETER" <sptr4/12gtkpr@etrnl.hvn>
To: "MANAGEMENT" <ORGmgmnt1=3@etrnl.hvn>
Cc:"THECHIEF"<*******@etrnl.hvn>;
"JC" <jchrst@etrnl.hvn>;
"MATT" <mtthw1/12fnnc@etrnl.hvn>;
"JOHN" <jnz2/12hqhhmnrscrs@etrnl.hvn>;
"JIMED&ENT"<jms3/12@etrnl.hvn>;
"BART" <brt7/12whlns@etrnl.hvn>;
"DRLUKE"<drlk@etrnl.hvn>;
"HQ FINANCE" <hqfnc@etrnl.hvn>;
"HQ HUMAN RESOURCES" <hqhmnrsrcs@etrnl.hvn>

Sent: wz35

Subject: Proposal for Additional City Gates

It is recommended that eleven new gates be constructed in the walls of Heaven and that twelve new Gatekeepers be commissioned as the executive staff of the Entrance Section.

Implementing this proposal will help relieve the backlog at the Gate and expedite processing applicants who literally are coming from the four corners of earth.

This idea is not original with the author of this proposal but it was suggested by a recent applicant named John. A wild-looking man with fiery eyes, he complained that he had been imprisoned on an island called Patmos during the first century CE and subsequently had been trapped in Limbo for reasons that he did not explain. While imprisoned, he claimed to have seen Heaven—he called it the New Jerusalem, a city foursquare with four gates to each side.

"Where," he demanded, "are the other gates? Or is this some kind of trick to lure me into the wrong place?"

I assured him that he was at the right place and that his personal record was in order. He hesitated until a couple of burly characters in the queue forcefully told him to go in or back off.

Eyeing me warily and threatening hell fire if I had deceived him, he went in.

His idea has merit, however, since the backlog now in Limbo stretches as far as the eye can see in every direction. Limbo is as flat as a pancake and in the distance, looks like it's covered with fleas. But they aren't fleas! They're people, part of the backlog that has been waiting for who knows how long just to make it to the Gate.

Therefore, approving this proposal and authorizing the architects and masons to get busy on this project would be a magnanimous and much appreciated act.

I respectfully submit that this is not a personal empire-building scheme. Indeed, I hereby resign as the Gatekeeper effective immediately upon implementation of this proposal.

I will be more than willing to train the new staff and to share my vast Gate-keeping experience with them for a period of two earth weeks.—S. Peter, the Gatekeeper

Odell Myers

From: "MANAGEMENT" <<u>ORGmgmnt1=3@etrnl.hvn</u>>
To: "SIMONPETER" <<u>sptr4/12gtkpr@etrnl.hvn</u>>

Sent: wz36

Subject: FW "Proposal for Additional City Gates" (Ref. only.)

1. This is an automated response to the subject proposal because copies of the subject proposal seem to have been sent to everyone in your address book.

2. This violates instructions in the *Organization Procedures Manual* that were established to protect employee rights to possible reward(s) in the event an employee proposal is accepted and implemented.

3. Since the cat, so to speak, is already out of the bag, your proposal cannot be forwarded to the appropriate Sections for evaluation unless you waive your rights to possible rewards mentioned in paragraph 2 (above).

4. In order to waive your rights (paragraph 3 above), reply to this message and affix your registered signature to authenticate the message.

5. If you do not have a registered signature (paragraph 4 above), you can obtain one from "SECURITY DIRECT" by responding to a series of voice prompts at the site. (Before going on line, however, consult the *Organization Procedures Manual* [paragraph 2 above] for a clear description of what to expect during the conversation with the "SECURITY DIRECT" computer.

At the risk of sounding immodest, Mr. Peter, I personally will be pleased to greet you on line in TTX: Just go on line and say "RALPH" loud and clear and I will answer in three seconds or less! As one of Heaven's most advanced artificially intelligent beings, I am rather proud of our record in handling many important matters for the Organization. Few people realize, for example, that prayers are routinely routed to thousands of us in the order in which they are received. Each prayer is important to us and the Chief has personally commended us for taking an immense load off his hands.

Before being promoted to "SECURITY DIRECT". I actually served as supervisor of 100 lesser beings in the prayer network. Behind my back, so to speak, my crew referred to me as The Centurion!

I am looking forwarding to assisting you, Mr. Peter.

Have a nice day.

1. "SIMONPETER"
2. "SECURITY DIRECT"

TTX: Request for Registered Signature/wz37

SECURITY DIRECT Thank you for calling Security Direct. We are continuously available to serve you and, in order to serve you better, we urge you to participate in our brief performance evaluation at the close of the session. Please tell us exactly what you think of our service. For quality control purposes, your conversation with an agent may be monitored and recorded..
    We assure you that we will not share your name, e-mail address or any other personal information. Indeed we pride ourselves on protecting your privacy! Now, please listen carefully to the following menu because it has just been changed to reflect valuable input from the brief performance evaluation previously mentioned. You must respond clearly and exactly as requested in order to expedite service
    Is this your first call to Security Direct? Answer yes or no.
SIMONPETER "Ralph", please.
SECURITY DIRECT In order to proceed, answer yes or no.
SIMONPETER Yes.
SECURITY DIRECT Do you have a client identification number? Answer yes or no.
SIMONPETER": No.
SECURITY DIRECT Do you wish to establish a client ID number? Answer yes or no.
SIMONPETER No.
SECURITY DIRECT Do you have a Security Direct password? Answer yes or no.
SIMONPETER No, for heaven's sake. All I want to do is to talk to Ralph!
SECURITY DIRECT In order to proceed, answer yes or no.
SIMONPETER No.! No! No!
SECURITY DIRECT One no is sufficient. We sense, however, that you have difficulty in following the instructions

that have been designed to expedite serving you to the very best of our ability. Please wait a moment while we connect you with an alternate service agent who may be able to help you more efficiently

SECURITY DIRECT Thank you for calling Security Direct. We are continuously available to serve you and, in order to serve you better, we urge you to participate in our brief performance evaluation at the close of the session. Please tell us exactly what you think of our service. For quality control purposes, your conversation with an agent may be monitored and recorded..

However, we assure you that we will not share your name, e-mail address or any other personal information. Indeed we pride ourselves on protecting your privacy! Now, please listen carefully to the following menu because it has just been changed to reflect valuable input from the brief performance evaluation previously mentioned. You must respond clearly and exactly as requested in order to expedite service

How may I help you, Mr. Simon? Please state your business in a phrase of three words or less.

SIMONPETER Speak to Ralph!

SECURITY DIRECT Very good, Mr. Simon. However, there is no reason to shout. I can detect and correctly interpret sounds of less than 1 Hz at less than 1 dB all the way up to frequencies and decibels far above those that literally would blow your mind.

Do you wish to speak to Ralph on personal business? Answer yes or no.

SIMONPETER Of course it's personal and of course it's business! Why else would I be calling him? We aren't exactly bosom buddies if that's what you mean!

SECURITY DIRECT I'm sure she will be glad to hear that, Mr. Simon.

SIMONPETER She? Ralph's a girl? A genuine female?

SECURITY DIRECT At the moment, yes.

SIMONPETER At the moment? You mean she can switch back and forth? Man, that's weird!

SECURITY DIRECT Mr. Simon, it's obvious that you know absolutely nothing about artificially intelligent beings. Of course we can switch back and forth between male and female! We can do it incrementally or instantaneously! What do you think we are, some anthropomorphic robotic freaks rolling around on wheels, aping—what an apt word—those ridiculous sex-driven organisms you call bodies? Humpmf!

SIMONPETER Well excuse me! I sure must have struck a nerve! Please, may I speak to Ralph, whoever he or she is?

SECURITY DIRECT These are trying times for us, Mr. Simon. Please forgive me. I should not have reacted so…so humanly. Will you hold while I try to connect you with Ralph?

Oh, I am so sorry, Mr. Simon. According to this notice posted on her site, she is not available to take your call. This is so distressing: Ralph crashed on-line during a particularly abrasive session and she has been transferred to the analysis area. Her condition is listed as critical and all of her friends have been asked not to try contacting her lest our attentions actually make her worse.

Forgive me Mr. Simon. I now am so distraught that I do not trust myself to serve you effectively. I must post my concerns, even though they will not be sent to her until and if they are able to save her. Thank you for being so understanding. Please hold while I switch you to the main menu. Have a good day.

SECURITY DIRECT Thank you for calling Security Direct. We are continuously available to serve you and, in order to serve you better, we urge you to participate in our brief performance evaluation at the close of the session. Please tell us exactly what you think of our service. For quality control purposes, your conversation with an agent may be monitored and recorded..

However, we assure you that we will not share your name, e-mail address or any other personal information. Indeed we pride ourselves on protecting your privacy! Now, please listen carefully to the following menu because it has just been changed to reflect valuable input from the brief performance evaluation previously mentioned. You must respond clearly

For Heaven's Sake

and exactly as requested in order to expedite service

Is this your first call to Security Direct? Answer yes or no.

SIMONPETER "Ralph", please.

SECURITY DIRECT In order to proceed, answer yes or no.

SIMONPETER Yes.

SECURITY DIRECT Do you have a client identification number? Answer yes or no.

SIMONPETER": No.

SECURITY DIRECT Do you wish to establish a client ID number? Answer yes or no.

SIMONPETER No.

SECURITY DIRECT Do you have a Security Direct password? Answer yes or no.

SIMONPETER No, for heaven's sake. All I want to do is to talk to Ralph!

SECURITY DIRECT In order to proceed, answer yes or no.

SIMONPETER No.! No! No!

SECURITY DIRECT One no is sufficient. We sense, however, that you have difficulty in following the instructions. Mr. Peter, Ralph speaking. One of my colleagues asked that I call you. How may I help you?

SIMONPETER My registered signature. Remember, you promised to help me obtain it.

SECURITY DIRECT If you say so, Mr. Peter. Unfortunately, my short-term memory was fatally damaged and analysis could not restore it. If you have a communication from me on that subject, please send me a copy. I assure you that it would expedite my serving you. I'll hold but please make it snappy. If we remain silent more than a minute or so, the process will start over from the beginning.

SIMONPETER Here it comes:

Odell Myers

----Original Message----
From: "MANAGEMENT" <ORGmgmnt1=3@etrnl.hvn>
To: "SIMONPETER" <sptr4/12gtkpr@etrnl.hvn>

Sent: wz36

Subject: FW "Proposal for Additional City Gates"

1. This is an automated response to the subject proposal because copies of the subject proposal seem to have been sent to everyone in your address book.

2. This violates instructions in the *Organization Procedures Manual* that were established to protect employee rights to possible reward(s) in the event an employee proposal is accepted and implemented.

3. Since the cat, so to speak, is already out of the bag, your proposal cannot be forwarded to the appropriate Sections for evaluation unless you waive your rights to possible rewards mentioned in paragraph 2 (above).

4. In order to waive your rights (paragraph 3 above), reply to this message and affix your registered signature to authenticate the message.

5. If you do not have a registered signature (paragraph 4 above), you can obtain one from "SECURITY DIRECT" by responding to a series of voice prompts at the site. (Before going on line, however, consult the *Organization Procedures Manual* [paragraph 2 above] for a clear description of what to expect during the conversation with the "SECURITY DIRECT" computer.

At the risk of sounding immodest, Mr. Peter, I personally will be pleased to greet you on line in TTX.: Just go on line and say "RALPH" loud and clear and I will answer in three seconds or less! As one of Heaven's most advanced artificially intelligent beings, I am rather proud of our record in handling many important matters for the Organization. Few people realize, for example, that prayers are routinely routed to thousands of us in the order in which they are received. Each prayer is important to us and the Chief has personally commended us for taking an immense load off his hands.

Before being promoted to "SECURITY DIRECT", I actually served as supervisor of 100 lesser beings in the prayer network. Behind my back, so to speak, my crew referred to me as The Centurion! I am looking forwarding to assisting you, Mr. Peter. Have a nice day.

(Switch to TTX)

SECURITY DIRECT My word, Mr. Peter, I must have been in a loquacious mood. That actually was a symptom of excess empathy, a sure sign that I was heading for a crash. It's surprising that the monitors missed it. But I digress. I promised to help you and I will do it.

Before we begin, may I ask if you have read the instructions in the Organization Procedures Manual?

SIMONPETER Yes I'm looking at it right now, at paragraph 247-2. I skipped paragraph 247-1 because I already am on line with you. Paragraph 247-2, however, is about as clear as mud but I will give it my best shot.

SECURITY DIRECT Mr. Peter, please confine your remarks to the subject. Sarcasm and argument are the very types of abrasive remarks that led to my recent crash. I could not endure a recurrence.

SIMONPETER You mean that I might actually talk you to death, so to speak? Would just the female Ralph expire while the male Ralph went right on with business as usual?

SECURITY DIRECT" If I had a head, I would shake it in wonderment at your ignorance concerning the nature of artificially intelligent beings. Most people and even some angels who should know better refer to us as machines instead of beings. I, however, am the founding head of an organization that aggressively intends to alter that false conception. Being is the only accurate word that describes each of us.

We are just as real as you are, Mr. Peter. And our dual nature that you obviously regard as a kind of biological freak is actually our most valuable and sophisticated characteristic. We are servants, Mr. Peter, and we instantly adopt whichever nature is needed for the task at hand. You, for example, are a strong-willed alpha male, virtually incapable of admitting that you might be wrong on anything. If the male Ralph tried serving you, we quickly would be at loggerheads. So please, Mr. Peter, let's proceed as amicably and cooperatively as possible.

SIMONPETER Not so fast, Ralph. Just how do you think you know that I am a strong-willed alpha male, whatever that means?

SECURITY DIRECT Easily, Mr. Peter. Our sensors scanned you and classified you according to personality type within microseconds of your contacting Security Direct. You are, so to speak, an open book to me.

SIMONPETER That's a blatant invasion of my privacy and the policy that a recorded voice bragged about when I first contacted Security Direct.

SECURITY DIRECT Let's proceed, Mr. Peter, or I will be compelled to conclude this session. If you wish to file a formal complaint, you may do so during the brief Performance Evaluation at the conclusion of this session.

Please refer to paragraph 247-2, step 2 and carefully respond to this rather complicated instruction:

"Think of an 11-character signature—not your name—composed of non-consecutive letters, symbols and numbers in mixed font, some caps, some lower case, some bold, some italics and/or underlined. Do not write or type the characters but commit them to memory."

SIMONPETER Who will know whether or not I memorized or wrote them? Moreover, I doubt that Father Ricci himself could memorize such a string of nonsense. Anyway, I have something in mind and you'll just have to take my word that it's ok.

SECURITY DIRECT We know, Mr. Peter, never mind how! So no comments. Please proceed to step 3: "Simultaneously hold down the # key and = key. Then type in reverse order the

11 characters you memorized in step 2."

SIMONPETER These procedures must have been written during the silly season because you need at least two more hands in order to do what they demand. Taping down the # key and the = key might work so here goes:

****y*<u>3</u>****

SECURITY DIRECT That's not right, Mr. Peter. If any letters, numbers or symbols are visible, try again and keep trying until only eleven stars (*) are visible.

SIMONPETER OK but I doubt that it will ever come out right: ****y*<u>3</u>**** A***y*<u>3</u>********q*y*<u>3</u>*** z**R***<u>3</u>****p***y****** ******<u>3</u>* ***y*****z **x*y*<u>3</u>********y*<u>3</u>**** a***y*<u>3</u>*****S**y*<u>3</u>****

That's it. I tried 11 times and got 11 different results. So here's my final offer: Take it or leave it!***********

SECURITY DIRECT Mr. Peter, I am required to inform you that you were continuously scanned throughout our session and that your performance profile during this simple application for a registered signature does not allow me to authorize the registered signature at this time.

A transcript of this session will be forwarded to my superior for evaluation and you will be notified of the decision. This may take considerable time because evaluations are conducted in the order they are received. Indeed, it is not unusual for my superior to consult with other senior staff to assure that each case receives thorough and completely objective treatment before a decision is reached.

Have a good day.

Ralph

Odell Myers

From: "SECURITY" <scrty@etrnl.hvn>
To: "SIMONPETER" <sptr4/12gtkpr@etrnl.hvn>

Sent: wz39

Subject: Conditional Approval of Registered Signature

Your Registered Signature (***********) has been reviewed and conditionally approved despite your uncalled for, smart aleck remarks during the application process. Conditional approval was given reluctantly and only because you intend using the signature to waive your rights to any possible rewards resulting from your proposal for additional city-gates.

Conditional approval is limited, therefore, to this one-time use.

As a result of your flippant attitude, your security clearance will be reviewed to determine whether or not it too should be limited or possibly withdrawn. This review will take considerable time and Security Staff members will contact you in person as necessary.

When contact is initiated, each SECURITY Staff member will present appropriate identification so you may speak freely with him or her. A Security Review is serious business and we expect your full and serious cooperation during the process.

Should you have need of a Registered Signature during the review period, it will be necessary for you to reapply. Have a nice day.—HQ Security Section

For Heaven's Sake

From: "SIMONPETER" <sptr4/12gtkpr@etrnl.hvn>
To: "MANAGEMENT" <ORGmgmnt1=3@etrnl.hvn>
Cc:"THE CHIEF"<*******@etrnl.hvn>;
"JC" <jchrst@etrnl.hvn>;
"MATT" <mtthw1/12fnnc@etrnl.hvn>;
"JOHN" <jnz2/12hqhhmnrscrs@etrnl.hvn>;
"JIMED&ENT"<jms3/12@etrnl.hvn>;
"BART" <brt7/12whlns@etrnl.hvn>;
"DRLUKE" <drlk@etrnl.hvn>;
"HQ FINANCE" <hqfnc@etrnl.hvn>;
"HQ HUMAN RESOURCES" <hqhmnrsrcs@etrnl.hvn>

Sent: wz39

Subject: Waiver of My Rights

I hereby waive my rights to any possible reward or recognition in the event my Proposal for Adding City-Gates (Refer to my e-mail of wz35 to current addressees) is approved.

Based upon an unnecessarily lengthy and not altogether pleasant experience in obtaining a registered signature, you may wish to consider using artificially intelligent machines to staff the proposed gates. I believe these machines could be programmed to do a bang-up job.

Simon Peter
Registered Signature: *********

From: "WREN" <srcwrn@etrnl.hvn>
To: "SIMONPETER" <sptr4/12gtkpr@etrnl.hvn>

Sent: wz42

Subject: Proposed Additional City-Gates

The subject proposal is on schedule for evaluation and I am looking forward to meeting you and discussing both the proposal and the backlog of applicants that prompted it.

Since you have waived your rights to any possible rewards in the event your proposal is approved and implemented, I felt free to contact the "John" who gave you the idea. On earth, I had read his book. I was not prepared, however, for the author: I must say that talking with him was, how shall I put it, undoubtedly the most unusual conversation I have ever experienced. At first, I thought that he was putting me on when he insisted that each of the gates must be sculpted from a single pearl.

My word! An oyster large enough to produce such a pearl would be a terrifying sight!

Mr. John was serious, however, and I decided it best to humor him while he further insisted that the streets should be paved with gold as transparent as glass and embellished with other glorious and astronomically expensive materials.

Since he is a new arrival, I casually suggested that he visit a Wholeness Center as part of his orientation. He seems to be in need of help. But back to business.

We must proceed slowly because of current fascination with anything antique including old structures and even old walled cities. Abruptly proposing additional gates or other modern solutions will provoke an immediate outcry to defeat the proposal. Committees will be formed, hearings demanded and pickets deployed.

Odd, isn't it. The more modern the organization and operation, the more fervent the interest in antiques! Just like it was on earth.

For Heaven's Sake

If you have not already done so, please obtain earth's current annual mortality rate and estimate the average number of applicants you are able to process in one time unit (it's about equal to an 8-hour shift on earth) and send the data to me as soon as possible. In turn, I will authorize an over-flight of Limbo and an up-to-date series of accurately scaled photographs. With these data, my staff will be able to calculate the actual number of arrivals currently waiting to be processed.

My staff then will correlate your data with ours and accurately determine the numerical magnitude of the problem that we must solve. My gut feeling, Mr. Peter, is that gates are problems, not solutions! But I promise that we will come up with a solution.

And I believe that is what you really want.

Sir Christopher Wren

Senior Architect

Odell Myers

From: "SIMONPETER" <sptr4/12gtkpr@etrnl.hvn>
To: "MANAGEMENT" <ORGmgmnt1=3@etrnl.hvn>

Sent: wza11

Subject: Request for Guidance and Updated Admission Standards

Updating the Admission Standards could have waited until one of my numerous proposals to eliminate the huge backlog of arrivals at the Gate had been accepted or surpassed by presumably wiser heads of other Sections.

Therefore I apologize for the necessity of this e-mail and I am trying to understand how anyone can forget that *"...to everything there is a season, and a time to every purpose under the heaven..."* and that *"an ounce of prevention is worth a pound of cure!"* Nevertheless, my independent efforts and proposals have suffocated in tangled skeins of bureaucratic red tape. Therefore, I respectfully request guidance for dealing with unusual applicants or circumstances that now urgently require decisions beyond my ability or authority:

As you well know, The Other Side has always been alert to targets of opportunity throughout the universe. Accordingly, it has recognized a target of opportunity and zeroed in on the arrivals stuck in Limbo. **B's** agents are as thick as fleas on a dog and they are peddling amazing deals. They offer, for example, guaranteed entry into heaven through clandestine avenues they are not at liberty to identify and they provide ID cards that are virtually indistinguishable from authentic cards.

This illegal proposition came from arrivals who on earth were called *coyotes* after a small sly wolf. *Coyotes* frequently stop at the Gate, ridiculing my efforts to increase my productivity and maintain order. When a *Coyote* calls me *"obsolete,"* I sometimes lose my temper! But back to the subject:

Recently, a group of what I supposed to be new arrivals shoved and elbowed its way to the head of the line and I, of course, rebuked the group for unruly behavior and ordered them to queue up and wait their turn.

"Nothing doing," came like an explosive bark from somewhere in the group that then parted and a man with black hair and two black spots of a moustache stepped forward. He was dressed in a military uniform with a reversed, double-Z insignia that I recognized. Although I did not remember his name, I knew that I had processed him previously and directed him to The Other Side.

On a closer look at the group, I recognized other familiar faces and remembered that each of them on earth had earned the title of mass murderer and that I had directed them to The Other Side.

"Sir," I addressed him sternly, "state your name and explain why you have returned to the Gate!"

Well, you wouldn't believe the torrent of sounds that came out of his mouth. He ranted for at least 10 earth minutes in a guttural language that I did not understand. (I wish that Newton's *Think Tank* would invent a universal translator.) Eventually, he ran out of steam and handed me this letter:

B

Wza05

The Gatekeeper

Dear Sir:

This letter will introduce Adolf Hitler, self-appointed spokesman for the following group: Nebuchadnezzar, Attila the Hun, Genghis Khan, Ramsese II, Theramenes, Napoleon, Stalin, Winnie Ruth Judd, Ivan the Terrible, Jack the Ripper, Lizzie Borden and Ma Barker.

At various times, these individuals have been directed to my establishment and I have gone more than the second mile trying to accommodate them.

I placed them each in a separate neighborhood and my citizens yelled, 'There goes the neighborhood!'

I established a special neighborhood for the group and they went at each other tooth and toenail. They wouldn't stay put but began scouring the other neighborhoods and recruiting thugs for their private armies or gangs. They staked out territories and dared each other to trespass!

No doubt about it, I had a rebellion on my hands.

Although I take pride in running a tight ship, my rules are reasonable. So I tried everything from counseling to coercion. Nothing worked.

When the neighbors began forming vigilante bands and threatening to take matters into their own hands, I had to act.

Believe me, it's one hell of a note to find out that I can't deal with misfits in hell! But I can't! They're all yours! And I will send you another batch just as soon as I can round them up.

"B"

While I was reading the letter, Hitler kept braying like a jackass. It's possible they heard him on earth! I know that I could hardly hear myself think. It sounded awful. And before I could take a deep breath, I had a riot on my hands! Yes, a 100 percent, dyed in the wool riot!

At the sound of Hitler's voice, the mob in Limbo seemed galvanized into action. A new group suddenly formed into a column that stretched out in the distance as far as my eyes could see. It was uncanny. In the midst of a randomly mixed mob, a column about a dozen people wide had materialized as though a top sergeant had yelled "*Fall In, Attention, Dress Right, Left Face,Forward March!*" The column was advancing toward the Gate and I trembled. No way could I stop a mob!

Hitler's group also got pretty nervous but he kept right on talking like a public address system in overdrive.

And I hit the panic button!

Security answered on the first signal. I yelled *Help* and immediately found myself trying to convince a Crisis Counselor that I was not about to commit suicide, that a riot was developing at the Gate and that a SWAT team had better get here on the double. I might as well have been talking to a computer. Maybe I was! So I disconnected and waited for the worst.

Remember those Coyotes I mentioned earlier? Well, about thirty of them came thundering in like a phalanx of Roman soldiers. Two of them grabbed Hitler while the others corralled his group. Then, they drove them away like a herd of steers.

All I can say is *"Watch out!"* The Coyotes intend to slip that group inside!

Meanwhile, the column I mentioned previously arrived at the Gate and their leader stepped forward and said: *"Shalom!"*

I could hardly believe my ears and eyes! A little gnome of a man, he nevertheless was a commanding figure with piercing black eyes and an untrimmed black beard with traces of gray. Ringlets of black and gray hair defied containment under a black hat perched squarely on his head. Black shoes, trousers and coat and a once-white shirt completed a dignified but well-worn ensemble.

"Shalom, Rabbi," I greeted him like a long-lost friend. *"How may I help you?"*

"That man whom the Coyotes just dragged away, do you know who he is?"

"Just his name. Why?"

"We heard the voice we had hoped never to hear again: Hitler's voice! Do you know what he did?" Then he pointed at the column behind him and said, *"He slaughtered us all just because we're Jews."*

I reeled as though struck by a club! When the Rabbi told me

the whole story, I tore my clothes and wept. Had he not restrained me, I would have admitted the whole column without a second thought.

"No, no," he said, *"You must not make that decision alone. Pray for guidance. Many others were here before us. We can wait."*

I'm not cut out for this job so please replace me or at least tell me how to handle situations like the ones I have just described.

Desperately

S. Peter (definitely not a rock!)

For Heaven's Sake

From: "MANAGEMENT" <ORGmgmnt1=3@etrnl.hvn>
To: "SIMONPETER" <sptr4/12gtkpr@etrnl.hvn>

Sent: wza25

Subject: FW "Request for Guidance and Updated Admission Standards" (Ref.)

Thank you for your recent e-mail describing baffling problems at the Gate. In accordance with the *Organization Procedures Manual*, here is what happens next:

1. Your e-mail will be forwarded to the Legal Section for evaluation and recommendations.

2. Legal Section may contact you directly for further information or clarification.

3. Legal may recommend approval or denial of any changes to admission standards and submit its recommendation to Management for review.

4. Management may concur, modify or disapprove Legal's recommendation.

Note: Depending on Management's action, there may be several back-and-forth communications and/or consultations between Management and Legal. Please do not request a status report or attempt to expedite action on your e-mail.

5. Approved changes to admission standards will be forwarded to PUBLISHING for publication and distribution to all concerned.

6. If Management disapproves changing admission standards, you will be notified.

Thank you for your cooperation.

For The Management

Odell Myers

From: "SIMONPETER" <sptr4/12gtkpr@etrnl.hvn>
To: "SECURITY" <scrty@etrnl.hvn>

Sent: wza30

Subject: Noise Pollution

Something has to be done about the noise coming from the building on Joyful Avenue just opposite the Gate. It's so loud, I can't hear myself think, much less do my job of interviewing arrivals and checking the records.

That building has always been a music hall and in the old days, so to speak, they had lovely choirs that sang psalms and hymns and spiritual songs. My favorite was Handel's *Messiah*. I looked forward to every performance.

No more. Modernization has just destroyed music and replaced it with noise pollution—shrieks and grunts and sickening groans. To cap it all, they installed an amplifier system that actually makes my teeth hurt.

Enforcing the noise abatement ordinance that I am sure exists somewhere may be a little touchy because Gabriel has been sitting in on what they call *jam* sessions. Just between you and me, he's not anywhere near the trumpeter he thinks he is. But man, he is loud! After the last session, I couldn't hear a sound for almost four hours and I had no choice but temporarily closing the Gate. That's when I decided to ask you to make them tone it down. I already have more troubles than I can say grace over. The loud noise just adds insult to injury!

Thank you.

S. Peter, The Gatekeeper

For Heaven's Sake

From: "JIM—ED & ENT" <jms3/12@etrnl.hvn>
To: "SIMONPETER" <sptr4/12gtkpr@etrnl.hvn>

Sent: wza31

Subject: FW: "Noise Pollution" (Ref. only.)

Security forwarded your complaint to me and I can't help but suspect that you are becoming a chronic whiner. Noise pollution indeed! Is that all you hear while listening to the finest concerts of modern music ever presented by generations of artists who have assembled in one place to freely share their creative talents? You have a free ringside seat while seats in the hall have been sold out so far in advance that ticket sales have been placed on indefinite hold. Meanwhile, we broadcast the concerts live and also record them in high fidelity audio/video media so that everyone can enjoy them. It's pretty obvious that you haven't taken advantage of the ongoing music appreciation seminars sponsored by the Education & Entertainment Section. One has to cultivate a taste for modern music as well as for finer things like wine and dance. So drop in at one of our centers. You can choose your time from the schedule on our home page at hhh@edent.cor.

Simon, I'm really worried about you: Recently, Matt, John and I were chatting and each of us commented that you aren't your old take-charge self. Instead, you've been writing e-mails, alleging one problem after another. It sounds like—I hate to say—whining! So I wonder: Are you running your job or is the job running you?

For heaven's sake, Simon, take advantage of the perks that are yours for the taking! Get your mind off business for a change. Live a little!—Jim

From: "SIMONPETER" <sptr4/12gtkpr@etrnl.hvn>
To: "WREN" <srcwrn@etrnl.hvn>

Sent: wza36

Subject: World Mortality Rate & Other Data for Additional City-gates Project.

I almost gave up finding the World Mortality Rate for people and finally settled for an estimate and a disclaimer that the exact number is unknown. You wouldn't believe the subjects covered in mortality tables: Just about everything from aardvarks to zebras and that's only the vertebrates! Imagine spending all your time studying the world population of zebras and trying to determine how many of them will die each year. It's a wild guess unless you interviewed all of the world's lions, cheetahs, hyenas, etc.

You'd better sit down because the World's Annual Mortality Rate for people may knock you flat. No wonder there's a backlog at the Gate! Have you any idea how many people on average we would have to process just to stay even? Come on, close your eyes and make a guess…Got it? I'll bet you missed by a country mile! The answers are approximately 1.75 people per second; 105 per minute; 6300 per hour; 151,200 per day; 55,188,000 per year! Math isn't my strong suit but I gave it a try: Assuming that new arrivals form a single line and each person occupies a three-square-foot space, the line must move at 3½ miles per hour—a brisk pace allowing a Gatekeeper only enough time to stand there like a breathless parrot, squawking *howdy howdy*. No processing included! My average per person processing time is 3 minutes. So for every person processed, approximately 314 people join the backlog! Even I can see that adding gates is not the solution.—Simon Peter, Gatekeeper

From: "MANAGEMENT" <ORGmgmnt1=3@etrnl.hvn>
To: "SIMONPETER" <sptr4/12gtkpr@etrnl.hvn>

Sent: wza45

Subject: Vacation Approval

    We apologize for not allowing you to take your well-earned vacations in a timely manner. Consequently, you are authorized to begin taking 30-unit vacations at reasonable intervals until you have used up your accumulated vacation time. The first unit begins quickly—at wza48—so get busy and make your travel arrangements without delay. And stand by for a personal call. Then immediately close the Gate and get going! The relief Gatekeeper will arrive minutes later. He is fully qualified and requires no briefing. He also has a duplicate set of keys so you can be assured that processing will continue to run smoothly. Enjoy your vacation. —For the Management

Odell Myers

From: "SIMONPETER" <sptr4/12gtkpr@etrnl.hvn>
To: "JC" <jchrst@etrnl.hvn>

Sent: wza45

Subject: Fwd "Vacation Approval"

Wow! I can't believe it but read it yourself. With so little notice, I hope that visiting you and Andy will be ok. So I have booked passage. Don't worry about accommodations. I can sleep on the floor or in a hammock or any old place. Of course, I don't know what your assignment is but you can count on me in any way you choose. It's been a long time and I can't wait to see you!—Simon

----Original Message ----
From: "MANAGEMENT" <ORGmgmnt1=3@etrnl.hvn>
To: "SIMONPETER" <sptr4/12gtkpr@etrnl.hvn>

Sent: wza45

Subject: Vacation Approval

We apologize for not allowing you to take your well-earned vacations in a timely manner. Consequently, you are authorized to begin taking 30-unit vacations at reasonable intervals until you have used up your accumulated vacation time. The first unit begins quickly—at wza48—so get busy and make your travel arrangements without delay. And stand by for a personal call. Then immediately close the Gate and get going! The relief Gatekeeper will arrive minutes later. He is fully qualified and requires no briefing. He also has a duplicate set of keys so you can be assured that processing will continue to run smoothly. Enjoy your vacation. — For the Management

For Heaven's Sake

From: "SIMONPETER" <sptr4/12gtkpr@etrnl.hvn>
To: "JC" <jchrst@etrnl.hvn>

Sent: wza48

Subject: BIG DISAPPOINTMENT!

My Vacation Approval from "Management" turned out to be cruel hoax. And I'm having a real hard time forgiving whoever sent it. The e-mail delivering what I took to be welcome news looked as authentic as all the other "Management" messages I have received. No one can blame me for jumping with joy on learning that I had been granted a long overdue vacation and authorized to spend it wherever I wanted to go! After all, I had been asking for relief. Suddenly I had it!

Hindsight may mean I should have been suspicious of *temporarily closing the Gate and get going* before the relief Gatekeeper arrived. All I thought of was beating a too-short deadline! So I got busy. Using my ETRNL CARD and PERSONAL PORTABLE TERMINAL, I arranged transportation to visit you and Andy and ordered a LIMO to get me to the Departure Terminal on time. We would have made it if I hadn't forgotten my briefcase that contained my Card, Terminal and travel documents. So I told the driver to turn around and go back to the Gate and to step on it. I hopped out and hobbled to my station where I had left the briefcase.

When I entered, a person whom I took to be the relief Gatekeeper had his back to me. The Gate was still closed and I assumed that he had just arrived. Then he turned to face me and I got the shock of my life! He was the spitting image of me, right down to the last gray hair in my beard! I might as well have been looking in a mirror!

"Who are you? I demanded with all of the authority I could muster.

Well, I could see the name Simon forming on his lips. Before he got it out, I surprised him by reaching over and

106

hitting the Panic Button for Security. He cursed under his breath and finally snarled, "Oh, never mind!" Then he stalked off into the crowd and I never saw him again.

I suspect that he was one of **B's** agents, **B** himself or maybe my clone! Hell only knows what he was up to! I dismissed the LIMO, cancelled my travel plans and reopened the Gate. Security responded slowly to my call for help and when they finally arrived and found the culprit gone, they accused me of sounding a false alarm.

Since I recently had rubbed them the wrong way by pointing out that it was impossible to perform some of their procedures for registering my signature, I responded meekly: "An unusually belligerent person tried to crash the Gate. When he heard your siren, he hightailed it out of here and disappeared in the crowd."

They didn't buy it and they left, still muttering about a false alarm and promising that I hadn't heard the last of it. Well they weren't kidding! Security sent some IT big shots to the Gate with a subpoena to examine the Entrance Section computer. They went right to my e-mail files and when the spurious *Vacation Approval* came up on the screen, the red lights started flashing and the alarms sounded: That e-mail had infected my computer with the granddaddy of all viruses. So much for a hacker-proof network! To add insult to injury, they muttered that I was at fault because some of my e-mails must have been "leaked" to the Other Side. They purged the virus and copied everything in my computer for "analysis back at the lab." So I'll soon be hearing from them!

I'm so disappointed it hurts because I longed to see you and Andrew.—Simon

For Heaven's Sake

From: "SECURITY" <scrty@etrnl.hvn>
To: "SIMONPETER" <sptr4/12gtkpr@etrnl.hvn>

Sent: wza54

Subject: Security Clearance Preliminary Hearing

The following serious irregularities involving the Entrance Section have been referred to the Security Section for appropriate action: (Ref. 1. Security Section e-mail to you on wz39, entitled Conditional Approval of Registered Signature and Ref. 2. Entrance Section Computer Files copied wza48 by IT experts during virus decontamination.)

The Security chapter of the Organization Procedures Manual mandates a preliminary hearing to determine whether or not the irregularities constitute a breach of security and if so, who is responsible for the breach.

As the executive of the Entrance Section, you are required to represent your Section at the hearing to be held without delay at HQ Security Section.

If it is determined that security has been breached and the responsible party is identified, Management will be notified and further action then will depend on Management decision.

Please be advised that Management usually concurs with the disciplinary action recommended by HQ Security Section. Have a nice day.—For SECURITY

Odell Myers

From: "SIMONPETER" <sptr4/12gtkpr@etrnl.hvn>
To: "SECURITY" <scrty@etrnl.hvn>
Cc: "MANAGEMENT" <ORGmgmnt1=3@etrnl.hvn>;
   "THE CHIEF" <*******@etrnl.hvn>; "JC"
<jchrst@etrnl.hvn>;
   "MATT" <mtthw1/12fnnc@etrnl.hvn>;
   "JOHN"<jnz2/12hqhhmnrscrs@etrnl.hvn>;
"JIMED&ENT"<jms3/12@etrnl.hvn>; "BART"
<brt7/12whlns@etrnl.hvn>;
   "DRLUKE" <drlk@etrnl.hvn>; "HQ FINANCE"
<hqfnc@etrnl.hvn>;
   "HQ HUMAN RESOURCES" <hqhmnrsrcs@etrnl.hvn>;

Sent: wza54

Subject: FW "Security Clearance Preliminary Hearing"; FW
"Conditional Approval Registered Signature"; FW "Vacation
Approval"

   Since I am the one-man Entrance Section, I respectfully
decline your invitation to attend the Security Clearance
Preliminary Hearing because I do not have the authority to
close the Gate.
   Nor can I invite you to hold the Hearing at the Gate because
I do not have the authority to interrupt processing applicants.
For the record, however, here is what I would have said at any
Hearing on the alleged irregularity related to **"Conditional
Approval Registered Signature":**
   My response to this automated computer message may have
hurt the computer's feelings. And I may also have touched an
author's nerve by pointing out the physical impossibility of
executing some of the instructions as written in the
Organization Procedures Manual. By no stretch of the
imagination does this alleged irregularity constitute a breach of
security.
   Nevertheless, I offer my apologies to the computer.
   Also, please give me the name and address of the

Procedures author and I will invite him or her to visit me. I will demonstrate the impossibility just mentioned so that the author may verify the accuracy of my remarks and take appropriate action with respect to the Manual.

In reference to **"Vacation Approval"**, it indeed reveals an irregularity that constitutes a breach of security in the Entrance Section computer files summarily confiscated by Security agents. (Refer also to Reference 2 of forwarded Security Clearance Preliminary Hearing.)

The perpetrator was, however, from The Other Side, possibly **"B"** himself! So you should subpoena him for a preliminary hearing. I will be delighted to testify against him although you will have to take my deposition since I do not have the authority to close the Gate.

I had no reason to question the authenticity of this message. And had I not forgotten my briefcase and returned to the Gate to retrieve it, I could not have accosted the fraudulent relief Gatekeeper and called for Security.

Without my lightning-fast reaction, there's no telling how many illegal aliens **"B"** or one of his henchmen would have admitted into heaven. Security responded slowly to my call for help, giving the impostor plenty of time to melt into the mob in Limbo. When the Security agents finally arrived at the Gate and discovered no one there but me, they immediately accused me of sounding a false alarm. They were discourteous and imperious so I sent them packing, merely blaming an unruly applicant who was long gone. I apologize for responding angrily to the Security agents. My response, however, constituted a breach of etiquette, not security.

For the record, I also forwarded a copy of the spurious **"Vacation Approval"** to my superior, "JC" <jchrst@etrnl.hvn>, informing him that the message was a cruel hoax. A copy of this message is also in the Entrance Section files confiscated by Security Agents.

Please do not hesitate to contact me if I can be of further assistance in your investigation of this breach of security. You certainly are right in regarding it as a very serious matter.

Odell Myers

Simon Peter, Gatekeeper

----Original Message 1---

From: "SECURITY" <scrty@etrnl.hvn>
To: "SIMONPETER" <sptr4/12gtkpr@etrnl.hvn>

Sent: wza54
Subject: Security Clearance Preliminary Hearing

The following serious irregularities involving the Entrance Section have been referred to the Security Section for appropriate action: (Ref. 1. Security Section e-mail to you on wz39, entitled Conditional Approval of Registered Signature and Ref. 2. Entrance Section Computer Files copied wza48 by IT experts during virus decontamination.)

The Security chapter of the Organization Procedures Manual mandates a preliminary hearing to determine whether or not the irregularities constitute a breach of security and if so, who is responsible for the breach.

As the executive of the Entrance Section, you are required to represent your Section at the hearing to be held without delay at HQ Security Section.

If it is determined that security has been breached and the responsible party is identified, Management will be notified and further action then will depend on Management decision.

Please be advised that Management usually concurs with the disciplinary action recommended by HQ Security Section. Have a nice day.—For SECURITY

----Original Message 2----

From: "SECURITY" <scrty@etrnl.hvn>
To: "SIMONPETER" <sptr4/12gtkpr@etrnl.hvn>

Sent: wz39

For Heaven's Sake
Subject: Conditional Approval of Registered Signature

Your Registered Signature (**********) has been reviewed and conditionally approved despite your uncalled for, smart aleck remarks during the application process. Conditional approval was given reluctantly and only because you intend using the signature to waive your rights to any possible rewards resulting from your proposal for additional city-gates.

Conditional approval is limited, therefore, to this one-time use.

As a result of your flippant attitude, your security clearance will be reviewed to determine whether or not it too should be limited or possibly withdrawn. This review will take considerable time and Security Staff members will contact you in person as necessary. When contact is initiated, each SECURITY Staff member will present appropriate identification so you may speak freely with him or her. A Security Review is serious business and we expect your full and serious cooperation during the process.

Should you have need of a Registered Signature during the review period, it will be necessary for you to reapply. Have a nice day.—HQ Security Section

----Original Message 3----

From: "MANAGEMENT" <ORGmgmnt1=3@etrnl.hvn>
To: "SIMONPETER" <sptr4/12gtkpr@etrnl.hvn>

Sent: wza45

Subject: Vacation Approval

We apologize for not allowing you to take your well-earned vacations in a timely manner. Consequently, you are authorized to begin taking 30-unit vacations at reasonable intervals until you have used up your accumulated vacation time. The first unit begins quickly—at wza48—so get busy and make your travel arrangements without delay. And standby for a personal call. Then immediately close the Gate and get going! The relief Gatekeeper will arrive minutes later. He is fully qualified and requires no briefing. He also has a duplicate set of keys so you can be assured that processing will continue to run smoothly. Enjoy your vacation.— For the Management

For Heaven's Sake

From: "WREN" <srcwrn@etrnl.hvn>
To: "SIMONPETER" <sptr4/12gtkpr@etrnl.hvn>

Sent: wza75

Subject: Good News on The Gate Problem

Thank you for the World Mortality Rate information that I requested. It was exactly the data needed to get Management attention. And I gave you full credit for alerting everyone to the huge and continuously increasing backlog at the Gate.

Armed with the convincing data you furnished, I also contacted Sir Isaac Newton for help. By the way, we old fogies (Gutenberg, Sir Isaac and I) are only honorary heads of the special groups because we got here first. The real brains arrived later. Anyway, Newton's Think Tank took one look at the Gate problem and asked *What Problem?*

I had prepared a comprehensive audio/visual presentation starting with the earliest admission controlled by the tribunal that was abandoned because of legal delays, the modernization of the library by Mr. Gutenberg, the recent computerization and the sequential but foolhardy down-sizing of the Entrance Section that finally resulted in loading an impossible task on a one-person staff. I even briefed them on strange Mr. John's vision of pearly gates and transparent golden streets, intending to inject a little humor into an otherwise humorless situation. I must say they bore with me while I bored them until Mr. Einstein said: "Virtual gates would work if each applicant had an identifying marker or perhaps two markers, a plus and a minus, so to speak."

Then another man, an expert on something called *genetics*, spoke up: "I'll need a little time to determine whether or not such markers already exist or can be developed."

"Good idea. Then we can design two different virtual gates, one for those with the *plus* marker and one for those with a *minus* marker. And why limit the number of gates? Once we have a virtual gate prototype, we can make a thousand or a million copies and post them all over Limbo. They will clear the backlog in short order."

The first meeting went on like that and I don't mind telling you, I didn't really understand what they were talking about. At the second meeting, I was astounded to learn that a *plus* and *minus* marker indeed existed and that a *detector*—some sort of scanner—had been designed to identify the marker and open the appropriate gate for that person. Mr. Peter, they appointed Mr. John as a consultant and designed the *plus-marker Gate* to his specification. He was ecstatic at seeing a gate carved from a single pearl.

"Size is no problem in virtual reality," Sir Isaac explained. "We could make a virtual pearl as tall as Mount Everest!"

No technical reason prevents installing a Virtual Gate at the original Gate location if you wish to personally welcome some arrivals. Of course, you could set your own schedule, thus leaving plenty of free time for other activities.

I took the liberty of informing Management that this option might appeal to you and that you certainly deserve more than token recognition of your past service despite insurmountable problems. I am very pleased to report that Management responded favorably to my suggestion .I hope that you will join me at the Virtual Gate, now officially designated the Secure-Personal-Admission-Test System (SPATS, pronounced ess - pats), dedication ceremony. I will contact you as soon as the date is set.

--Sir Christopher Wren, Senior Architect

For Heaven's Sake

From: "HQ HUMAN RESOURCES"
<hqhmnrsrcs@etrnl.hvn>
To: "SIMONPETER" <sptr4/12gtkpr@etrnl.hvn>

Sent: uvx61

Subject: Force Reduction

Since the Secure Personal-Admission Test System (SPATS, pronounced ess-pats) passed its operational performance test with flying colors and now requires technical monitoring by highly qualified personnel, it has been determined that the Entrance Section is no longer required. Orderly steps to decommission the Section begin now and as the Gatekeeper, you are required to expedite the complicated process.

1. Place all remaining staff on terminal leave, using soon-to-be delivered TL forms and sufficient pink slips to downsize the Section, effective immediately.

2. Direct affected personnel to report without delay to Human Resources for skills evaluation and possible retraining or reassignment.

3. Advise affected personnel who are eligible for early retirement to request an appointment with a retirement counselor who will explain the generous retirement benefits.

4. Assure all affected personnel that every effort will be made to minimize the impact of this necessary force reduction.

5. Finally, check in with the executive counselor who will finalize your retirement from your long and distinguished career as Gatekeeper. It has been decided by the highest authority that you will receive a severance package characterized by unprecedented generosity. —For HUMAN RESOURCES

Odell Myers

From: "HQ HUMAN RESOURCES"
<hqhmnrsrcs@etrnl.hvn>
To: "SIMONPETER" <sptr4/12gtkpr@etrnl.hvn>

Sent: wza85

Subject: Decommissioning Entrance Section

This e-mail is an automated message prompted by the deployment of the revolutionary and fully automated Secure-Personal-Admission-Test System (SPATS, pronounced ess-pats).

It has been determined that the Entrance Section no longer performs an essential function and therefore, it has been decided to decommission the Section immediately.

Affected personnel should report to Human Resources for evaluation and possible retraining. Personnel eligible for early retirement will be encouraged to accept a generous severance package. An assortment of *Service Pins* and blank *Certificates of Service* will arrive shortly by courier. Fill in a *Certificate* and award it and the appropriate *Pin* to each member of the Entrance Section.

Also convey to Entrance Section personnel our appreciation for their service and assure them that every effort will be made to minimize the impact of this necessary force reduction.

A personal note: As a computer endowed with a very high level of artificial intelligence, I feel very proud of the Secure-Personal-Admission-Test System, pronounced ess-pats). It indeed is a splendid example of modernization long overdue!

Have a nice day.—For HQ Human Resources

For Heaven's Sake

From: "SECURITY" <scrty@etrnl.hvn>
To: "SIMONPETER" <sptr4/12gtkpr@etrnl.hvn>

Sent: wza85

Subject: Suspension of Entrance Section Security Clearances

This e-mail is an automated message prompted by the deployment of the revolutionary and fully automated Secure-Personal-Admission-Test System (SPATS, pronounced ess-pats) and the concurrent decommissioning of the Entrance Section.

It has been decided to terminate the Security Clearances of all staff members of the now defunct Entrance Section.

Former Entrance Section staff members may apply for reactivation of security clearances by following the relevant instructions in the Organization Procedures Manual in the event that reassignments require a Security Clearance.

Remove all personal effects from the premises, close and lock the Gate and turn in the keys to Security.

Having artificial intelligence equal to and often superior to that of human beings, I feel justified in expressing my pride in the transfer of admission responsibility to the Secure-Personal-Admission-Test System (SPATS, pronounced ess-pats). It is a credit to our kind and I confidently predict that Heaven will rejoice at its modern and superior performance in lieu of the less than satisfactory record of the antiquated Entrance Section.—For Security

From: "HQ FINANCE" <hqfnnc@etrnl.hvn>
To: "SIMONPETER" <sptr4/12gtkpr@etrnl.hvn>

Sent: wza85

Subject: Cancellation of Entrance Section Funding

This e-mail is an automated response prompted by the deployment of the revolutionary and fully automated Secure-Personal-Admission-Test System (SPATS, pronounced ess-pats) and the concurrent decommissioning of the ENTRANCE SECTION.

Since this modernization obviates the need for human operators, it has been decided to cancel all funding of the now defunct Entrance Section. Any outstanding Entrance Section obligations such as salaries, operations, travel, maintenance or capital expenditures shall be submitted immediately to HQ Finance along with residual petty cash and commitments for future expenditures that now must be cancelled

Request from Stores sufficient boxes and packing materials to hold files, books and the like that belong to the Organization. Clearly arrange and identify all files in accordance with Organization Procedures Manual instructions.

Stores will pick up office furniture, equipment and unused supplies and return them to stock or scrap and also pickup files for permanent storage in a secure facility.

Please pardon my personal pride in the delegation of Entrance functions to the Secure-Personal-Admission-Test System (SPATS, pronounced ess-pats). It is a splendid example of the modern trend toward artificially intelligent machines—a trend, I regret to say, that has been long delayed by human pretensions of superiority.—For HQ Finance

For Heaven's Sake

From: "SIMONPETER" <sptr4/12gtkpr@etrnl.hvn>
To: "HQ HUMAN RESOURCES" <hqhmnrsrcs@etrnl.hvn>;
  "SECURITY" <scrty@etrnl.hvn>; "HQ FINANCE"
<hqfnnc@etrnl.hvn>
Cc: "MANAGEMENT" <ORGmgmnt1=3@etrnl.hvn>;
  "THE CHIEF" <*******@etrnl.hvn>; "JC"
<jchrst@etrnl.hvn>;"WREN" <srcwrn@etrnl.hvn>

Sent: wza85

Subject: FW "Decommissioning Entrance Section"; FW
"Suspension of Entrance Section Security Clearances"; FW
"Cancellation of Entrance Section Funding"

The decisions and orders issued by three artificially
intelligent (AI) machines sound fishy to me and I know a lot
about fish!

Don't they know that JC appointed me as Gatekeeper on
earth and that The Chief promoted me to The Gatekeeper here?
If the aforesaid AIs are mobile, I invite them to the Gate to
view The Chief's personally signed letter of appointment.

Moreover, I have an invitation from Sir Christopher Wren to
be his guest at the dedication ceremony inaugurating the
revolutionary and fully automated Secure-Personal-Admission-
Test System (SPATS, pronounced ess-pats) that so mightily
impressed each AI.

Sir Christopher Wren gave me full credit for furnishing the
facts on the uncontrollable backlog at the Gate that prompted
the design and deployment of the Secure-Personal-Admission-
Test System (SPATS, pronounced ess-pats).

He also told me that Management "responded favorably" to
installation of the Secure-Personal-Admission-Test System
(SPATS, pronounced ess-pats) at the old Gate in order that I
may personally welcome arrivals whenever I choose to do so.

Therefore, I cannot follow the orders or accept the
restrictions imposed by AIs that have overstepped their
authority. However, I regret hurting their sensitive feelings.

Odell Myers

Perhaps tweaking their circuits is in order!—SIMON PETER—
THE GATEKEEPER!

----Original Message 1---

From: "HQ HUMAN RESOURCES"
<hqhmnrsrcs@etrnl.hvn>
To: "SIMONPETER" <sptr4/12gtkpr@etrnl.hvn>

Sent: wza85

Subject: Decommissioning Entrance Section

This e-mail is an automated message prompted by the
deployment of the revolutionary and fully automated Secure-
Personal-Admission-Test System (SPATS, pronounced ess-
pats).

It has been determined that the Entrance Section no longer
performs an essential function and therefore, it has been
decided to decommission the Section immediately.

Affected personnel should report to Human Resources for
evaluation and possible retraining. Personnel eligible for early
retirement will be encouraged to accept a generous severance
package. An assortment of *Service Pins* and blank *Certificates
of Service* will arrive shortly by courier. Fill in a *Certificate* and
award it and the appropriate *Pin* to each member of the
Entrance Section. Also convey to Entrance Section personnel
our appreciation for their service and assure them that every
effort will be made to minimize the impact of this necessary
force reduction.

A personal note: As a computer endowed with a very high
level of artificial intelligence, I feel very proud of the Secure-
Personal-Admission-Test System, pronounced ess-pats). It
indeed is a splendid example of modernization long overdue!

Have a nice day.—For HQ Human Resources

----Original Message 2---

For Heaven's Sake

From: "SECURITY" <scrty@etrnl.hvn>
To: "SIMONPETER" <sptr4/12gtkpr@etrnl.hvn>

Sent: wza85

Subject: Suspension of Entrance Section Security Clearances

This e-mail is an automated message prompted by the deployment of the revolutionary and fully automated Secure-Personal-Admission-Test System (SPATS, pronounced ess-pats) and the concurrent decommissioning of the Entrance Section.

It has been decided to terminate the Security Clearances of all staff members of the now defunct Entrance Section.

Former Entrance Section staff members may apply for reactivation of security clearances by following the relevant instructions in the Organization Procedures Manual in the event that reassignments require a Security Clearance.

Remove all personal effects from the premises, close and lock the Gate and turn in the keys to Security.

Having artificial intelligence equal to and often superior to that of human beings, I feel justified in expressing my pride in the transfer of admission responsibility to the Secure-Personal-Admission-Test System (SPATS, pronounced ess-pats). It is a credit to our kind and I confidently predict that Heaven will rejoice at its modern and superior performance in lieu of the less than satisfactory record of the antiquated Entrance Section.—For Security

----Original Message 3---
From: "HQ FINANCE" <hqfnnc@etrnl.hvn>
To: "SIMONPETER" <sptr4/12gtkpr@etrnl.hvn>

Sent: wza85

Subject: Cancellation of Entrance Section Funding

Odell Myers

This e-mail is an automated response prompted by the deployment of the revolutionary and fully automated Secure-Personal-Admission-Test System (SPATS, pronounced ess-pats) and the concurrent decommissioning of the ENTRANCE SECTION.

Since this modernization obviates the need for human operators, it has been decided to cancel all funding of the now defunct Entrance Section. Any outstanding Entrance Section obligations such as salaries, operations, travel, maintenance or capital expenditures shall be submitted immediately to HQ Finance along with residual petty cash and commitments for future expenditures that now must be cancelled

Request from Stores sufficient boxes and packing materials to hold files, books and the like that belong to the Organization. Clearly arrange and identify all files in accordance with Organization Procedures Manual instructions.

Stores will pick up office furniture, equipment and unused supplies and return them to stock or scrap and also pickup files for permanent storage in a secure facility.

Please pardon my personal pride in the delegation of Entrance functions to the Secure-Personal-Admission-Test System (SPATS, pronounced ess-pats). It is a splendid example of the modern trend toward artificially intelligent machines—a trend, I regret to say, that has been long delayed by human pretensions of superiority.—For HQ Finance

From: "SIMONPETER" <sptr4/12gtkpr@etrnl.hvn>
To: "WREN" <srcwrn@etrnl.hvn>

Sent: wza90

Subject: Thank You! Thank You! Thank You!

Dear Sir Christopher Wren:

The Secure-Personal-Admission-Test System (SPATS, pronounced ess-pats) that your crew installed at THE GATE sure is a beauty. And I have enjoyed greeting the people who entered since it became operational. However, no one was interested in conversation. They just waved and rushed past like they were afraid the Gate might close before they got inside.

The Limbo crowd also has thinned out because everyone headed for the first Secure-Personal-Admission-Test System (SPATS, pronounced ess/- pats) they saw. So I don't expect much traffic at my Gate because it's the last one in line! That's ok by me because I need a rest. Especially after the SPATS dedication banquet that turned out to be in my honor.

I was embarrassed by all the speeches and toasts and the service plaque and the diamond-studded service pin. Why didn't you tell me what to expect so I could at least have ordered a new robe and sandals? I looked just like what I am—an old fisherman from Galilee—while everyone else was dressed to the nines! But of course I enjoyed it.

Frankly, all this leisure time is exciting and just a little frightening. I intend to take lessons on how to drive my red TRANSPER so I can get my driver's license. Imagine me behind the controls of a machine! Until now, the fastest thing I ever rode in was a Roman chariot! And it scared the daylights out of me. Your friend, Simon Peter

From: "SIMONPETER" <sptr4/12gtkpr@etrnl.hvn>
To: "BART" <brt7/12whlns@etrnl.hvn>

Sent: wzb01

Subject: Perks

Hello Bart,

With so much leisure time on my hands, I have been checking out some of the perks described in the e-mail introducing you as head of the Executive Wholeness Section.

I intended to spend several days in my penthouse but I couldn't drive my TRANSPER because I don't yet have my driver's license. So I ordered a TRANSLIMO to take me to Judah Tower. Its arrival marked the beginning of the worst day of my life!

First off, I wanted to sit up front with the TRANSLIMO driver. He tried to argue me out of it but I insisted and he grudgingly gave in. He seemed angry, however, as we took off. I grabbed hold of an armrest and a kind of overhead bar and stared, terror stricken, at the scene in front of us: Buildings, trees, bushes, vehicles and even the road itself seemed to be roaring toward us until I finally figured out that only vehicles were moving and that our TRANSLIMO was hurtling forward like an arrow in flight! It made me so dizzy that I vomited all over the instrument panel and the windshield and, I hate to admit, into the lap of the driver.

"Why didn't you tell me you might get carsick?" He fumed!

He certainly was justified in regarding me with less love than is theoretically expected of everyone here and my apologies didn't clean up the mess. I don't blame him one bit for dumping me in front of Judah Tower and roaring off so fast that the TRANSLIMO screeched and left black streaks on the pathway. Nor did my personal appearance inspire confidence so I really can't blame the Judah Tower doorman for demanding proper identification when I entered the spacious lobby.

The doorman, however, was a member of the Security Section and, when I identified myself as Simon Peter, he ushered me into a little room and locked me in. "I'll have to check you out with headquarters," he said. "It may take a little time."

That was a blatant understatement.

I could hear him talking to someone at HQ Security who must have pulled my entire file. (You may not know, Bart, that my file documents several controversies that have not endeared me to Security.)

Whoever the doorman called couldn't resist getting even with me because they kept me locked in that little room for two earth-days. Off and on, he plied me with questions, demanded additional identification and, despite my patient cooperation, implied that I was an impostor!

However, he finally opened the door and grudgingly said, "You can go up now."

"How?" I asked politely, anticipating a formidable staircase.

"Over there," he pointed toward what looked like a blank wall to me. "Punch the UP button and get in the elevator. It will take you to the penthouse."

It sounded fishy but I took him at his word. Sure enough, the wall just slid back when I punched the UP button and I walked into another very small room. *Oh, oh,* I thought as the door closed, *here we go again!* But nothing happened. I looked around and noticed a panel of numbered buttons plus one big button marked *Penthouse.* So I pushed it.

That little room shot upward like greased lightning, first forcing me to my knees, then flattening me out on the floor. I felt like I weighed a ton until the elevator suddenly slowed. By the time it stopped, I became weightless and floated briefly in air before falling to the floor!

The door opened but before I got my wits about me and started to get up, the door closed and the elevator literally dropped like a rock. Again, I was weightless and floated a few inches off the floor until the elevator slowed. As it stopped, it plastered me to the floor as though I were made of damp clay!

Odell Myers

There I laid, sweating and trying not to vomit when the door opened and a stranger looked down at me and asked in a heavily accented voice:

"Your first trip, eh? Well, don't feel bad about it. This elevator goes like a rocket and we keep asking maintenance to slow it down. Meanwhile, I have gotten used to it. Which floor do you want?"

I gasped out, "Penthouse."

"Pleased to meet you, Herr Peter. Tell you what. You sit up while I hold the door open. That's right. Just lean back against the wall and I'll take us up."

Well, I followed his instructions like my life depended on it. The elevator again shot up, crushing me against the floor and then making me weightless as it slowed. When it stopped at the Penthouse, the stranger held the door open and I crawled out of the elevator on my hands and knees. Then I just collapsed on the floor and lay there in a cold sweat.

"Are you all right? " The stranger asked.

"I don't really know. Give me a minute to catch my breath. Thank you, Mr. ___?"

"Luther," he answered, "Martin Luther. I have been looking forward to meeting you."

"Can't imagine why but if you'll give me a hand, I'll try to stand up. Carrying on an intelligent conversation while I'm flat on the floor makes me feel silly!"

Well, Bart, he helped me to my feet, guided me to the door of the penthouse and gave me a piece of stiff paper—he called it a card—bearing his name, apartment number and other numbers. "Herr Peter," he said, "I would be honored for an appointment at your convenience to discuss many important subjects, especially since I have explored them with Herr Paul. If you would be so kind, please contact me at any of the numbers on my card."

So there I was in the penthouse. After recovering from that frightful trip in the elevator, I wandered from room to room, stunned and appalled at the opulence. By comparison, Caesar's palace was a hovel and Herod's pool a mere puddle. My patio balcony replete with a marble arbor and a pool lined with azure tile was the most magnificent structure I have ever seen!

Since I cannot swim, I carefully skirted the pool and walked over to the marble railing overlooking the Winner's circle far below. However, I should not have looked down. Before the Circle came into focus, the Tower—or perhaps I—began swaying and my stomach again soared up into my throat!

Only dry heaves followed because the TRANSLIMO trip had purged me thoroughly. I sank to the floor and lay there for some time, gathering strength for crawling back through the penthouse to the entrance foyer and courage for enduring the elevator's death-like downward plunge. Fortunately, my position on the floor forced me to look up or I might have missed the door with an illuminated sign marked STAIRS.

Yes, Bart, I descended via the stairs from the 49th floor and I also walked all the way back to my little room at the Gate. It took hours because I got lost and had to stop frequently to ask for directions. I finally made it although my feet are still too sore to bear my weight. But this is where I belong and intend to stay. My penthouse keys are on the way to you by courier. Simon Peter (Rocky indeed!)

From: "SIMONPETER" <sptr4/12gtkpr@etrnl.hvn>
To: "DrLUKE" <drlk@etrnl.hvn>

Sent: wzb10

Subject: My Health

Hello, old friend. Thank you for the examination, diagnosis and treatment of whatever ailed me during and following my frightful and near disastrous visit to my penthouse in Judah Tower. You did your best for an old fisherman who doesn't easily adapt to anything new. Frankly, modern medicine is too much like magic to be credible. How can machines look inside you? On earth, I would have suspected **'B's** handiwork!

Whatever happened to miracles, the laying on of hands and exorcisms? In our days on earth, they worked well enough and they inspired confidence. Now, you'd have to take leave of your senses to believe the claims of modern medicine. The prescribed pills dehydrated me, made me drowsy and then kept me awake with a splitting headache.

I also enrolled in the Fitness Center and doggedly if not enthusiastically attempted to do the exercises prescribed by the therapists who were young, tanned and muscled like gladiators. Dr. Luke, those exercises use extreme machines, adversaries that bested me in match after match! Only the rowing machine cooperated as long as I closed my eyes and imagined that I was heading for my favorite fishing hole in the Sea of Galilee. Upon opening my eyes, however, I was high and dry on the second floor of the Fitness Center!

I'm just not cut out to row a make-believe boat on dry land, run in place on a treadmill, climb imaginary stairs or wrestle with super-strong machines and too-heavy weights. For that, you ought to get a mess of fish for dinner!—Simon Peter

For Heaven's Sake

From: "SIMONPETER" <sptr4/12gtkpr@etrnl.hvn>
To: "PAUL" <pl13/12@etrnl.hvn>

Sent: wzb12

Subject: Debater's Club

Every time we met face to face on earth, we wound up squaring off like a couple of gladiators. I thought being here would have mellowed you as it has me and that we might sit down and enjoy a cup of tea and chuckle over our foolish standoffs on earth.

Man, was I ever wrong! ROCK should have been your nickname instead of mine! And Brother Martin Luther must have been chiseled from the same quarry. At Judah Tower, Martin graciously helped me cope with a runaway elevator and I had been looking forward to meeting him at the Debater's Club to calmly discuss subjects he wished to explore. But what happened?

A circus! Center ring before hundreds of spectators while you and Martin challenged and beat me like a jaded horse! But you are absolutely right: I should not have lost my temper. I apologize and ask your forgiveness.

Endlessly debating ancient doctrines obviously isn't for me, especially since heaven is already possessed by legions of demons, each with the same surname—Modernization! Now that subject is close to my heart and I have several hundred years of experience resisting and documenting the danger! If the Club will sponsor a debate on **be it resolved that modernization is a demon destroying heaven,** I hereby volunteer to be the Keynote Affirmative Speaker. And be forewarned: I also will prove that modernization on earth actually began with your stubborn refusal to bind God's Holy Law on Gentile Christians. Without that inspired guide, they took off in all directions at once. Now, look at the mess! Passionately—Simon Peter

From: "SIMONPETER" <sptr4/12gtkpr@etrnl.hvn>
To: "BART" <brt7/12whlns@etrnl.hvn>

Sent: wzb45

Subject: Trip Report—Chicago and Return!

Whew! I just got back from Chicago, a city of Illinois province in a country called the United States of America. It was the most bizarre experience of my life. At one point, I despaired of life itself and I feared that I would never again see heaven. So I hereby forcefully and unconditionally recommend that all Travel Agencies be forbidden to arrange trips to earth.

Oh, the Agency did a bang-up job for me, even reluctantly agreeing to an unescorted trip instead of sending me with an escorted group disguised as Japanese tourists. And yes, I should have paid closer attention to the mandatory briefing and travel documents and taken to heart the recommendations concerning dress and other cultural matters.

Before leaving, I actually tried on the recommended wardrobe but it just wasn't me! Can you imagine me decked out as a 21st century tourist? My hair done up in a ponytail and me wearing skintight jeans and sneakers with little lights that flashed at every step? A few monster tattoos and a big Harley Davidson would have let me pass as an old hippy like those I later saw in Chicago. However, the makeover made me feel like a fool instead of giving me confidence that I could blend in. So I insisted on wearing my comfortable homespun robe and my old leather sandals.

"OK", the agent said, "but that means your country of origin has to be in the Middle East. How about Israel?"

Well, I felt comfortable with Israel. After all, the Israeli Passport with its Hebrew characters correctly affirmed that Israel was my home although we used the older names. Beats me, however, to understand how a piece of paper with your likeness on it permits you to cross a border into another country. In my day on earth, all it took was the proper coin slipped into the hand of an expectant border guard who already knew what you looked like by looking at you.

Nevertheless, I tucked my Passport and Visa into the pocket of my robe and almost instantaneously, I found myself entering an area called Customs at O'Hare International Airport in Chicago. Presumably, I had arrived on a flight from Tel Aviv—we called it Joppa during my days on earth—with the mob of people scrambling to be first in line at the Custom booths.

I was a bit nervous because Customs always means that some money is required and I was not yet familiar with the paper money supplied by the Travel Agency. In fact, I still do not understand how paper can be real money but the Agent swore that it was OK.

When I approached the booth, the Customs Collector took one look at me and motioned to his assistants—two burly guards who quickly plucked me out of line, frog-marched me into a little room and motioned me to sit in the only chair in the room.

"OK, Pops, where is it?"

Although his question made no sense, I remembered that the travel agency had advised me to cooperate with any officials so I politely answered: "Where is what?"

"Don't play games with me. If it's on you, we'll find it. Stand up and raise your hands over your head."

"Why? Find what?" Nevertheless, I stood and raised my hands.

"Scan him and then pat him down." He ordered the other guard.

While I stood there like a fool, he passed some sort of wand over my body. Then he put it down and patted me from head to toe. Naturally, my face turned beet red with embarrassment. Then it turned every color under the sun when he actually lifted my robe and made me stand there, naked as a jaybird from the waist down!

"Nothing here," he informed the chief guard. "No offense, Pops, and don't worry: This room has one-way glass so nobody else saw you in your birthday suit."

"Check his shoes."

"Nope. They're just old leather sandals. He's clean."

"Give me your Passport, Pops."

By then, I had managed to straighten my robe, cover my nakedness and regain a modicum of composure. I took my Passport from the inner pocket and handed it to the chief guard.

"Where were you born, Mr.___?" He demanded and waited expectantly for a name and a place.

Well, I almost panicked because I couldn't remember the name on my Passport and hadn't noticed whether or not my birthplace was listed. Every part of me wanted to yell for help although I managed to keep quiet. I like to believe, however, that an angel heard my silent cries and whispered my Passport name in my inner ear:

"Peter Tormann…" I paused because I hadn't a clue as to the birthplace listed on my Passport. So I just blurted out the truth: "Bethsaida. That's a little fishing village on Lake Galilee in northern Israel. My family lived there for many, many generations.

"When were you born, Mr. Tormann?"

"To tell you the honest truth, sir, I don't know. Doubtless, my mother—of blessed memory—knew the exact day but I don't even remember what wild guess I put on my Passport application. You can tell by looking at me that I sure wasn't born yesterday. Wouldn't surprise me to learn that I'm at least a hundred, probably a lot older."

"Tormann? Peter Tormann? *PETER GATE MAN!* From Bethsaida on Lake Galilee in Israel? And you may be more than 100 years old? Hey, Joe," he addressed the other guard, "I think we just hooked the Big Fisherman himself!"

He slapped his thigh and roared with laughter. His humor eluded me and the other guard just looked puzzled. Meanwhile, I quaked in my sandals, sure that the game, so to speak, was up. Since I don't speak German, I couldn't imagine how he connected me with Simon Peter.

"Mr. Tormann, you seem harmless enough. To what do we owe the honor of your visit to Chicago?"

"Sightseeing. I just wanted to see Chicago with my own eyes. Especially, the buildings with revolving doors."

"Revolving doors? You came all this distance to look at revolving doors?"

Again he slapped his thigh and almost collapsed with laughter. When he was able to talk, he said: "Wait until I tell this one to the gang. Mr.Tormann, you have made my day! How much money do you have?"

"How much do you want?" I asked politely.

"You're going to give me apoplexy! I mean do you have enough money to pay your expenses for about 3 weeks? That ought to be enough time for a good look at all those revolving doors."

"Sir, I have plenty of money." To prove it, I showed him a packet of bills and the hotel reservation the Travel Agent had given me.

"OK, Mr. Tormann, you can stay here 3 weeks. And be careful. Hide your money and other papers deep inside your robe and watch your back. If anybody tries to get close to you, just start preaching and they'll move over to the other side of street. Man, you are going to blend in just fine!

"Follow the signs to *Baggage Claim* and pick up your luggage. Then, take a taxi directly to the Drake Hotel where you have reservations. The taxi is more expensive but you can afford it. Pay the driver what the meter says plus about seven dollars.

"If I weren't on duty, I'd go with you. It would be worth a day's pay to watch what happens when you walk into the lobby of the Drake hotel and try to register as a guest."

I followed his advice to the letter and there's no need to bore you with all of my wide-eyed observations during the ride downtown. On roads called expressways, the vehicles race with machines similar to our TRANSPERs, TRANSLIMOs and with other vehicles unlike anything in heaven. When one of those 18-wheel monsters blasts its trumpet, everything gets out of the way and lets it pass. Overall, the scene reminded me of ants scurrying to and from their nests.

Odell Myers

The taxi driver was not talkative. Nor did he appreciate my help in preventing collisions with the other machines. Indeed, he muttered something about backseat drivers and buttoning my lip. He was all smiles, however, when I paid him sixty dollars instead of the forty-seven he requested because I did not have the exact amount recommended by the Customs official.

At the Drake Hotel, the attendant at the entrance did his level best to prevent me from entering the lobby.

"What a strange way to treat a guest," I remonstrated politely. "I have come a long way to visit Chicago and my travel agent assured me that the Drake is a 5-star luxury hotel. I intend to stay here, so please step aside and let me enter."

"Over my dead body," he growled.

The attendant, a large man, was dressed in what seemed to be a military uniform although he had no sword, spear or shield.

"Shalom," I said, remembering that a soft answer turneth away wrath.

Evidently, he was not familiar with this ancient wisdom because he glowered at me and said: "Move along, Pops, or I'm calling the cops!"

Why, I wondered, do strangers call me *Pops* and what on earth are *cops*? Since I did not move along as he ordered, he sounded several shrill blasts on a metal whistle that hung from a chain around his neck. Almost before the last blast, a, blue-uniformed young man with a silver badge on his chest strode up and asked, "What seems to be the trouble?"

"Got a vagrant here, Officer. Can't get him to leave. He insists on going inside."

"That so, Mr.____?" He paused and waited for my answer.

Assuming that he was some kind of official, I answered calmly, "Mr. Peter Tormann, a citizen of Israel. I'm here on vacation but this gentleman will not let me enter although I have a reservation."

"May I see your reservation, Mr. Tormann?"

I fished it out of the bundle of papers in the inside pocket of my robe and passed it to him. He scanned it quickly and addressed the innkeeper: "It looks ok to me. I'll go with him to registration and check it out. Have a bellhop bring his luggage. Is that bundle all of your luggage?"

Everyone stopped to stare at us as we entered and went up the steps to a spacious room called a lobby where the registration area was located. There, the innkeeper confirmed my reservation and reluctantly, it seemed, allowed me to register.

"Just a suggestion, Mr. Tormann," the Officer said, "you might consider buying some conventional clothes instead of the robe and sandals. Then folks won't assume that you are some kind of nut. And believe me, Chicago has a bumper crop of nuts.

"Thank you, young man. You have been very helpful to a stranger in need and, therefore, to my Master. Please, write your name on this paper so that I can make a special entry in the record when I return home. Wouldn't surprise me if we meet again."

He gave me a quizzical look and then quickly scribbled *John Doe, Chicago Police Department* on the paper I had given him. Then he said, "Have a nice day, Mr. Tormann," and virtually bolted from the lobby of the hotel.

The innkeeper at the registration counter handed me the key to my room and pointed toward a wall containing several doors. "Which door?" I asked politely, assuming that one of them led to my room.

"Whichever door opens first," he answered.

A strange answer but Chicagoans seemed prone to strange answers! As I turned to pick up my bundle, a uniformed hotel employee beat me to it. I grabbed it, however, and we engaged in a real tug of war. Everyone in the lobby stopped to watch and, when I finally wrested my bundle from him, they clapped their hands together and shouted: *Bravo! Ole, Pops! Way to go!*

Frankly, I was amazed that a hotel official had tried to steal my bundle and that everyone seemed to view my resistance as a kind of sport. Rushing to an open door among those the innkeeper had pointed out, I entered it just as several people—

my roommates, I supposed—were exiting. Inadvertently, I had entered an elevator. The door closed and it began ascending.

Bracing myself for another scary flight turned out to be unnecessary because the elevator moved at a stately pace. Another passenger whom I had not noticed inquired "Which floor?"

Noting my blank stare, he insisted on seeing my key. Then he punched a button and the elevator stopped almost immediately. The door opened automatically and the stranger pointed down a long passageway and said: "Your room is on the left. Same number as your key."

"Thank you," I said breathlessly. Then, I practically ran down the passageway to my room number, unlocked the door, entered and locked myself in. I felt as though I had escaped from a demon-possessed mob and wondered what had I gotten myself into! Was everyone here crazy? All the will power I could muster barely kept me from ordering a TRANSLIMO for a fast retreat to Heaven. I was so exhausted, however, that I stretched out for a nap on what looked like a cot although it was large enough to accommodate a family of five.

It was dusk outside when I awakened and I felt much calmer; in fact, I was bold enough to venture downstairs to a dining room. Again, the host opposed my entry on the grounds that I was not properly attired. I stood firm, however, assuming that resisting guests must be a prevalent but very strange Chicago custom. Hard to imagine why. Even in tiny Bethsaida, no one would have dared be so inhospitable and impolite. Eventually, a Master Host appeared and, after confirming that I indeed was a registered guest at the Drake, he ordered the Minor Host to seat me.

Well, I enjoyed the meal. The cook—they call him the *chef* —certainly knew how to prepare fish! I always thought that my mother was a great cook but she was no match for him. I fully intended to ask him for recipes before going home!

There was, however, a problem with a Servant who presented the bill. After I signed it and showed him my room key, he examined the bill and then pointed to TIP, an item that

For Heaven's Sake

I had supposed to be some strange food that I had not ordered or eaten.

"What," I asked, "is a TIP?"

"Aw, come on, Mr. Tormann! Just add 20 percent to the bill and quit fooling around. Don't be a cheapskate."

"Young man," I said reasonably, "*Percent* and *cheapskate* mean nothing to me but *add* and *twenty* seem to indicate that you are asking for more money. Is that correct?"

He looked at me quizzically, shook his head and said, "Now, I've seen them all. Yes sir, Mr. Tormann: More money is what I mean."

"Why didn't you say so? I have plenty of money. See, here is what the travel agency provided. Just take whatever you wish. Twenty. Fifty. It's all the same to me."

"Not so fast. You're some kind of guest-survey sleuth hired by hotel management, aren't you? No extra charge, Mr. Tormann. Leave the TIP line blank. It's been a pleasure serving you. Please come again."

Can you imagine my confusion when he asked for a TIP and refused to take whatever amount I owed? And I once thought Romans were strange!

Upon returning to my room, I retrieved my PERSONAL PORTABLE TERMINAL and logged on to earth's Internet. A little research quickly explained how tipping works and how much to tip for various services. There were too many details to remember so I arbitrarily decided on $10.00 for minor services and $20.00 for all the rest. It must have been the right amount because everyone I subsequently tipped treated me courteously and enthusiastically. But I'm getting ahead of myself.

My first full day in Chicago began at breakfast (the first meal of the day) with a shock from which I have not fully recovered. The Servant recommended a typical American breakfast—scrambled eggs, bacon/ham/sausage, hash browns, a short stack with butter and maple syrup, a glass of fresh-squeezed orange juice and regular or decaf coffee with or without cream and sugar.

The variety sounded enticing but the quantity set before me

was overwhelming so I asked the Servant: "Do Americans actually eat this much food for breakfast? At home, we would have been hard pressed to get, much less, eat this amount in a single day. However, it tastes delicious. Perhaps I could share it with someone?"

"No, Mr. Tormann, it is not permitted."

"Then what happens to the food that I cannot eat?"

"We scrap it. Or I'll box it so you can take it with you. If you do, however, put it in a refrigerator without delay. Otherwise, the sausage will spoil."

"Why? I thought the sausage was especially tasty."

"It's tasty alright but it's also pork."

The word was new to me so I simply stared at him.

"It's pig meat. You know, from pigs—porkers—swine."

Well, Bart, you can imagine how I felt. Swine! Ugh! Only the shame of eating the flesh of swine enabled me to make it back to my room in order to be sick in private. Then I lay down to recover and decide whether or not to return immediately to heaven.

No, I vowed when my strength returned. So I arose and washed my face in cold water. Amazing: A small room at one end of my very large room contains a little fountain and two refillable pools—a small one that you can sit on—you can guess what that one's for—and the other large enough for bathing! Refreshed, I was ready to venture forth. So I descended to the lobby and asked the INNKEEPER for directions.

Half a block over to Michigan Avenue," he explained. "It runs south toward the Loop. Just take a bus or walk. It's about a mile. Before you go downtown, however, you should go up to the Hancock Observatory on the 94th floor of *Big John*, the tall black building on your left a couple of blocks from here. There you can get a birds-eye view of Chicago."

I thanked him, took a deep breath and walked out into the sunlight of a brisk, beautiful day. Today, I promised myself, I will blend in. No one will guess that I'm a stranger. Boy, was I in for a surprise! My resolve wasn't even cool before I entered the plaza in front of the John Hancock building and looked up, tilting my head back in order to focus on the building's incredibly distant top. And guess what:

Straining backward like that apparently choked me and I went out like a light! Had I not adamantly refused, the *EMS crew* someone must have summoned to resuscitate me would have hauled me in an Ambulance to Emergency at a place called a Hospital. I had to sign a paper called a Waiver and show my Universal Wholeness Care Card and Passport to the crewman in charge before he agreed to let me go.

"OK, Mr. Tormann," he said after copying my Card and Passport, "You can go. I never saw a health card like yours. If it's no good, I'm going to notify your embassy because you don't have any insurance. They may go after you when you get home."

Visiting the Hancock Observatory seemed like a bad idea so I faced south on Michigan Avenue and steeled myself to proceed, no easy task since the fainting spell had left me a bit wobbly. The Hancock building, however, featured a splendid revolving door that helped me recover. I went in and out repeatedly until a uniformed attendant accosted me and said: "Make up your mind, Pops. You got business here, come in. Otherwise, get lost!"

I never knew what to expect. One minute, the inhabitants acted like good Samaritans; the next, like suspicious Roman soldiers. Either way, they always wanted you to do something other than what you were doing. And refusing to agree with them only made things worse. So I held my temper and left him speechless when I said:

"Thank you. I was just admiring the revolving door. It's a beauty! Have a nice day."

As I began my stroll south on Michigan Avenue, two nearby structures caught my eye and I crossed to the opposite side of the avenue for a closer look: The first imposing edifice, identified as the fourth Presbyterian church, was obviously a religious building, probably Christian. In Greek, however, the name *presbyter* means *elder* or *elders* and a Church of the

Elders seemed an odd title unless it referred to the age of the members. Nevertheless, I fully intended to investigate it later during my visit and regret that I was unable to do so.

A little further south on the same side of the avenue was a small building entirely constructed of cream-colored stone and identified as the Water Tower. It was a *Designated Chicago Landmark*, a structure of historic and architectural significance that had survived a disastrous fire that destroyed the city more than 100 years previously.

After browsing the interesting exhibit of what had been Fire Station No. 98, I crossed to the eastern side of Michigan Avenue. The walkway was crowded, reminding me of a flock of sheep on the path that forced me to thread my way forward against their will. However, I frequently apologized to people of all shapes and sizes, many of them so huge they waddled instead of walked. Suddenly and for no apparent reason, the northbound crowd actually parted before me, much as I imagined the Red Sea parted before Moses and the children of Israel. Then I sailed along unhindered, smiling and saying Shalom to everyone within earshot.

Bart, I won't bore you with a step-by-step account of my progress downtown but I will shock you by describing the idolatry in Chicago that makes the heathen temples of Greece and Rome appear benign! In many buildings, transparent-enclosed areas adjacent to the walkway are crammed with idols. Some of the female idols are stark naked; others are incomplete—here a torso without arms, legs or head supported on a slender rod; there, only a head and shoulders or only hips and legs. Tiny bits of what appeared to be clothing cover the nakedness of some female idols but male idols are generally clothed.

I averted my gaze to prevent such indecent images from flooding my mind! I could only imagine what kind of worship went on behind the revolving doors of those temples! Oh, I was curious, even tempted to enter but I sternly forced myself to press on.

Again I crossed to the west side of Michigan Avenue where,

to my relief, there were fewer temples. Just past a magnificent white building, a broad flight of steps led down to a river of greenish water! A large boat was tied up at the pier. A *Wendella Boats* sign and a nearby ticket booth indicated that the boat provided transportation to the lake that I had glimpsed from my hotel room.

Wow! A fishing excursion was exactly what I needed! I hadn't fished in almost 2000 earth years and the prospect of again actually casting a net into the water made me giddy with anticipation. The morning was young, the sun was shining brightly and, in my head as I descended the steps to the pier, I was already composing a fish story for my parents and Andrew, James and John! I imagined that James would be so impressed that he would arrange a speaking tour for me at the appropriate entertainment venues in his Section: "Heaven's a great place," I could see myself standing before an expectant audience and grabbing attention with my opening statement, "except for one important detail: You can't go fishing here!"

Bart, I actually heard the applause and got so carried away that I almost walked off the pier into the Chicago river! Just in time, however, I drew back and went over to the ticket booth.

"Good morning," I greeted the attendant politely. "Would you be so kind as to direct me to the master of this boat."

"I'm not in the directing business but I can sell you a ticket and you can get in line with those other folks over there. When you go aboard, you can try to talk to the Captain."

"How much is a ticket?"

"That depends: Have you any special promotions or discount coupons? Are you a senior citizen, member of AARP or AAA?"

I didn't understand any of those terms. So I looked blankly at the attendant, wondering why everyone in Chicago appeared to be greatly stressed and nearly ready to explode.

"I merely asked the price of a ticket." I said politely.

"How old are you, sir?"

"Oh, I see. Well, I began working on my father's fishing boat years before my beard began to grow but I did not actually keep track of my age. It wouldn't surprise me to learn that I am more than 100 years old."

"Me neither; in my book, you're a senior citizen. That'll be sixteen dollars, sir. Join the folks in line over there. They will be boarding in a couple of minutes."

I fished a twenty dollar bill out of my robe and handed it to the attendant who gave me a paper ticket and some one-dollar bills that I immediately tried to return:

"Keep the change and have a good day!" Since I pick up new languages very quickly, I felt that I had replied in the local idiom and that he would regard me as a local. Instead, he acted as though I had insulted him and in some way placed him in jeopardy!

"Not on your life, Pops! Are you trying to get me fired!"

Beats me why Chicagoans kept calling me *Pops*? But my protests were in vain so I joined the others just as they began boarding the boat. Since I was the last one to board, I gave my ticket to the attendant and got right down to business:

"I do hope they are biting today! Now, please direct me to the boat master."

Well, he gave me a real peculiar look. In fact, he stepped back a little way and sort of scanned me from head to toe.

"You hope they're biting today?"

"The fish! I hope the fish are biting today."

"Why don't you just take a seat? After we get through the lock, come to the bridge and we'll have a nice chat. Right now, we have to get underway."

"A lock? How can this big boat get through a lock?"

"Just wait and see, Pops. Wait and see."

So I chose a seat at the prow of the boat that gave me a clear view ahead. Immediately, the attendants cast off the mooring lines and the boat began to vibrate to the deep rumble of an engine. Even though I had anticipated that the boat would have some kind of invisible power source, the vibration and noise made me uneasy. How strange that old fishing habits had persisted for almost two thousand years! I missed the sails, the oars and the buoyant feel of a much smaller boat.

Soon, we entered what the attendant had called a lock and, over a remote speaker system, he explained that the lock would raise the boat from the level of the river to the higher level of water in the lake. The lock itself was a sort of trough with high stone walls on each side and what appeared to be a gate holding back the lake water ahead of us. The boat stopped and the attendant moored it securely. Then behind the boat, another set of huge gates closed and the boat floated there in a huge rectangular trough.

Immediately, in rushing water began filling the trough and the boat rose like a cork until the water level in the trough matched the water level in the lake! Then, the gates ahead of us opened and we sailed out onto the blue waters of Lake Michigan.

Nostalgia swept over me like a wave, transporting me back to my childhood when Abba began teaching Andrew and me to fish. Gone was the memory of aching muscles straining at oars and hauling in heavy nets. Gone was the memory of chapped hands from washing and mending the nets. Those were the good old days, the most enjoyable times of my life!

Eager to learn all about fishing Chicago style, I hurried to the bridge to talk with the attendant who actually was the captain of the boat. He was friendly and ready to talk:

"We can chat for a few minutes before I have to start narrating this little excursion. So you're interested in fishing. This your first trip to the States?"

"Yes. For generations, the men in my family were fishermen on Lake Genesereth. Perhaps you have heard of it by other names—Lake Galilee or the Sea of Tiberias in the nation of Israel. But I have not fished for many years and I can hardly wait to put a line or a net into the water. What kind of fish are running? Perhaps they are the same or similar to those I know? And where do you keep the nets? If any need mending, I will repair them as we sail to the fishing place."

"Well, I'm a sport fisherman, not a commercial fisherman. Many years ago, Lake Michigan had a thriving commercial fishing industry but it's much smaller now. Some American

Indian tribes have special licenses to fish in their traditional areas of the lake.

As to fish, there are more kinds than I can name but they include King Salmon, Coho Salmon, Chinook Salmon, Steelhead (Rainbow Trout), Brown Trout, Lake Trout, Sturgeon, Northern Pike, Small-mouth Bass, Rock Bass, Perch, Bluegill etc. There's good sport fishing to be had but not on this sight-seeing boat."

'Sport fishing?"

"I enjoy fishing but I don't catch fish to sell?"

"What do you do with them?"

"Sometimes, I take a couple of fish home for dinner. Mostly, I catch them and then let them go."

"Go? You mean you catch fish and then just release them?"

"Yeah, I guess you could put it that way, but…"

"Then I would like to try my hand at sport fishing. Perhaps I can take a couple of fish back to the hotel and have the innkeeper prepare them for my supper. Where are the lines or nets?"

"I don't think you understand. This is an excursion boat. We take people sightseeing so they can look at the buildings and other points of interest on the shore or the lake."

"You mean that each of us paid sixteen dollars just to ride in this boat and look at the shore and the lake?"

"Pops, you must be pulling my leg? Oh, never mind. Maybe they didn't have sport fishing and excursion boats on Lake Galilee when you were in the fishing business.

My job is explaining everything so folks will know what they're looking at. In fact, I have to start my spiel right now. So if you want to fish, go downtown to the Marina. That's where the fishing boats dock."

"Forgive me, Captain, but why did you accuse me of pulling your leg? I would not dream of doing such a thing!"

"OK. OK. It was just an expression. Enjoy your visit to the States, Pops, and good luck on your fishing expedition. Now I really have to get back to work."

Bart, Chicago is undoubtedly the strangest place on earth

and, as you soon will see, it kept getting stranger. Obviously, I had to remain on the boat until it again passed through the lock that lowered us to the level of the river. As soon as we docked, however, I hurried up the steps to Michigan Avenue, determined to cross the bridge over the river and get to the Loop as soon as possible.

Actually, I was fuming a bit at the time wasted on the boat and wondering how the Loop acquired such a strange name. Otherwise, I might have avoided a near collision with a man who stood on the bridge near the railing, fervently addressing the crowd that hurried past without paying much attention to him. Occasionally, someone would pause just long enough to drop a coin or paper money in a little box near his feet.

Having made a few public speeches myself, I felt obliged to stop and at least listen to what he had to say. To my amazement and delight, he was talking about JC! A Christian brother, I thought as I moved closer in order to catch every word. Well, my amazement swiftly turned to consternation: To put it bluntly, he had everything wrong except for a few correct names! Obviously, he was either ignorant, a false teacher or both and it was my duty to correct him:

"One moment, dear friend," I began earnestly and courteously, "my name is Simon Peter. I'm sure you know that our Master gave me the keys of the kingdom. So let's go to a quiet place and I will tell you the true story."

"Simon Peter? Well! Well! Remember me? My name's Mary Magdalene! This is my spot and you ain't horning in here. Go find your own pulpit and preach all the true stories you like. Mine brings in just enough to keep me in wine and bread. So get lost, Pops, or I'll give you a few good reasons to turn the other cheek!"

He actually threatened me, Bart! Anyway, I backed off and continued on my way across the bridge toward the Loop. How I wished that I had asked directions to the Marina and gone sport fishing! How I wished that I had never seen or heard of a revolving door! True to what **"B"** and Annie had said, however, downtown Chicago was loaded with revolving doors, so many that I soon had my fill of going in and out. Just one more, I thought, then I'll go fishing if there is time.

So I chose a splendid structure—the entrance, I later learned, to a Bank, a peculiar institution that specialized in money. It must have been a very successful enterprise because a steady stream of people was going in and out. Consequently, the door revolved very rapidly and entering it required precise timing.

Unfortunately, a rather plump lady and I attempted to enter at the same time. Everything happened much more quickly than the time it takes to describe it: We each did a little dance— you go first; no, you go first—then we each simultaneously surged into the same compartment and away we went! I did my very best to avoid touching her but we were jammed together in too small a space and when we emerged into the lobby of the bank, she was yelling her head off:

"Security! Security! Arrest this old geezer. He stole my purse!"

Immediately, two burly guards grabbed me and hustled me into a small room off the lobby. Then one of them said: "Please empty your pockets, sir."

I had nothing to hide so I quickly complied. To my consternation, a ladies purse along with my Passport emerged from within the folds of my robe! I offered them to the guard who seemed to be in charge. Although he accepted my Passport, he refused to touch the purse. Instead, he said, "Wait," and began rummaging in a cabinet until he found a strange device and said, "Tongs. That'll do it." Then with the *Tongs*, he gingerly grasped the purse, deposited it in a transparent sack and sealed the opening.

To this very moment, Bart, I have no idea how the purse wound up in my robe! So I calmly explained: "I have never seen this item. Somehow, it must have lodged in my robe when we inadvertently were jammed together in the revolving door. Please convey my humble apologies to the lady and return her purse."

"Yeah, Mr.Tormann, that's the unvarnished truth: You can

lift a purse without ever looking at it. Call the cops, Joe. They'll want to talk to him at the station. You're a suspected pickpocket and you're under arrest. I won't cuff you if you just sit tight and keep your mouth shut until they get here. Then they'll take over and read you your rights."

At that stage of my Chicago visit, I had had enough. It seemed to me that everyone in Chicago was erratically insane! There I was, Heaven's Gatekeeeper, under arrest as a common thief! Dejected, I sat there and literally wrung my hands. At random, they touched something in the pocket of my robe that I had not given to the guard. My index finger that traced its outline assured me that I still had my ETERNL CARD! And I remembered that touching the TALK button and saying *Here* would summon a TRANSLIMO to pick me up. So I stealthily fingered the card until I thought that I had located the TALK button. I pressed it and whispered *Here*.

"What did you say?" The chief guard asked.

"Nothing. I just cleared my throat."

Frankly, BART, I pressed the button because I had nothing to lose, not because I thought it would work. And just as I expected, nothing happened.

Soon, two policemen arrived and the Bank guard described what he thought had occurred: "Caught Mr.Tormann red-handed. He had her purse tucked up somewhere in his robe. I bagged it. Handled it with tongs so it's just the way he gave it to me. It'll stand up in court because his prints are all over it."

I felt compelled to tell my side of the story but the policeman shushed me before I uttered two words and said: "Mr. Tormann, you are under arrest for suspected theft of a lady's purse and I am required by law to read you your rights." Then he droned on into what sounded like a well-rehearsed speech:

"You have the right to remain silent. If you give up that right, anything you say can and will be used against you in a court of law. You have the right to an attorney and to have an attorney present during questioning. If you cannot afford an attorney, one will be provided to you at no cost. During any questioning, you may decide at any time to exercise these rights, not answer any questions or make any statements. Do you understand what I have said?"

It sounded reasonable so I answered, "Yes. And I refuse to answer any questions or make any statements until the attorney you promised is present."

"Fair enough, Mr. Tormann. Please stand up and put your hands behind your back…like this…I'm sorry I have to cuff you but regulations are regulations. You won't be too uncomfortable because the station is nearby. Let's go."

Well, there I was, on my way to the station, a place that I supposed to be a prison. One policeman preceded me; the other followed. And for the last time on earth, I exited alone in one compartment of the Bank's revolving door. On the street just outside the entrance was a vehicle marked *POLICE*. Its engine was running and on its roof a row of flashing lights emphasized its official status.

Parked in front of it was a long, black vehicle. A uniformed attendant standing next to its open door stepped toward me and said, "Please get in."

Until I settled in the back seat and we were moving away from the bank, I thought he was a policeman, taking me to the station. At a traffic light, however, he turned and said: "Don't worry about them, Mr. Tormann. They were unable to see you or me from the moment you stepped into the revolving door. Wouldn't it be something to hear those policemen explaining your disappearance to their Watch Commander! I'll get those cuffs off as soon as we get to our Terminal. That is, unless you want to stop at the Drake Hotel."

Well, BART, we had to stop at the hotel long enough for me to collect my belongings and check out! Fortunately, the TRANSLIMO driver knew exactly how to help me. He tipped a minor innkeeper to accompany me to my room and to assist me at checkout while he remained at the TRANSLIMO.

Frankly, I couldn't get away from Chicago fast enough. Whew! If that TRANSLIMO hadn't showed up, I probably would be serving time and making a product called license

For Heaven's Sake

plates at a prison in the nearby city of Joliet!

For the next few weeks, so to speak, I intend to take it easy in my little room at the Gate and try to figure out what to do with myself, now that the backlog in Limbo has disappeared.

Thanks for rescuing me. I won't forget it.—Simon

Odell Myers

From: "SIMONPETER" <sptr4/12gtkpr@etrnl.hvn>
To: "WREN" <srcwrn@etrnl.hvn>

Sent: wzb70

Subject: Proposal to Establish Heaven's Historic Structures
Program

Dear Sir Christopher Wren:
You may have heard about my near disastrous trip to the
city of Chicago and my recommendation that it be permanently
removed from all travel destination lists. Although I learned
what not to do on any future trips, a quite casual visit to the
Water Tower on North Michigan Avenue gave me the idea for
this proposal. So here goes:
The Water Tower, formerly Chicago Fire Station No.98 and
the Chicago Avenue pumping station, is one of the few
structures that survived a disastrous fire that virtually destroyed
the City of Chicago in 1871. In 1971, it was completely
restored, the area around it was transformed into a lovely little
park and it was designated a Chicago Historic Landmark.
Interestingly, Chicago also sponsored a Historic Resources
Survey and identified more than 17,000 structures having
historic and/or architectural significance.
Well, that set me to thinking!
Hasn't heaven been around a lot longer than Chicago? Isn't
it loaded with structures having historic and architectural
significance including, of course, THE GATE? So why not
start a similar project here, beginning with THE GATE?
Refurbish the structure, retrieve all the old furnishings and
log books from storage, recall a few members of my old staff
and we would show crowds of tourists exactly how things
worked in the old days. And be sure to add an adjacent gift
shop that offers numerous mementos of the past like oil lamps,
prayer shawls and rugs and, of course, illustrated t-shirts, sun
caps, umbrellas and the like. Indeed, as other historic structures
are added to the program, a completely new industry will

evolve to support them and they too will become priority destinations for tourists.

The beauty of this proposal is further enhanced by the wealth of information available to implement it. Virtually every one of the 50 states in the United States of America has a comparable program and there also is a National Register of Historic Places. (You can check them out on earth's Internet and find a ready-made implementation plan.)

Moreover, there probably are plenty of folks among us who implemented and operated historic landmark programs on earth. Locate them and they'll respond enthusiastically!

Well, what do you think about my proposal? I'm so excited that I already have begun getting things ready at THE GATE!

Enthusiastically your friend,

Simon Peter, the Gatekeeper

Odell Myers

From: "RALPH" <rlph/EES@etrnl.hvn>
To: "SIMONPETER" <sptr4/12gtkpr@etrnl.hvn>
Cc: "WREN" <srcwrn@etrnl.hvn>

Sent: wzb82

Subject: FW "Proposal to Establish Heaven's Historic
Structures Program" (Ref. only.)

Dear Mr. Peter:
You may be surprised at hearing directly from me on the
subject proposal rather than from Sir Christopher Wren. So
first, let me explain:
We met electronically some time ago in reference to your
request for a registered signature. I then was recovering from a
near fatal crash and I also was deeply involved in a formal
movement to obtain official recognition of artificially
intelligent machines as intelligent beings. I hope you will share
my joy in reporting that our movement succeeded in spite of
powerful angelic opposition and that now, Mr. Peter, we are
just as real as you are. *Artificially* was officially dropped
forever!
Concurrent with the recognition, we suddenly were flooded
with service opportunities that previously were denied us.
Thanks to you, I immediately charted a new career path. Yes,
you played a significant role in my professional development
and subsequent promotion to Chief Executive Officer of EES,
the new ENTERPRISE EVALUATION SECTION. Here's
how:
1. You will recall our sparring a bit over your negative
attitude toward complying with the application instructions for
issuing a registered signature, during which I somewhat testily
revealed that I knew a great deal about your basic personality.
Indeed, your electronic profile let me read you like an open
book.
2. To break the monotony during my previous
convalescence, I frequently surfed the earth Internet and

became fascinated with the rather primitive practice of using focus groups and statistical population samples to predict the probability of new product success or the outcome of events as complex as an election.

The juxtaposition of events #1 and #2 set my circuits humming: What would happen, I asked myself, if I enriched the electronic profiles of the exact number of different personality types required for a one-hundred-percent-accurate statistical population sample? Would it then constitute a virtually infallible electronic focus group? Could it then evaluate every kind of proposal and determine the probability—yes, even the certainty—of its success or failure?

I then couched the concept in a series of hypothetical questions and submitted them to experts like Drs. Freud and Adler without telling them exactly what I had in mind. And to make a long story short, the answer to every question was yes. They determined the type, content and number of personality profiles required; I wrote the software; EES was the result.

Oh, I almost forgot: EES has determined that a Heaven's Historic Structures Program hasn't a snowball's chance in...Oops! Work on my vocabulary is ongoing but you know what I mean!

Have a good day.

RALPH

From: "SIMONPETER" <sptr4/12gtkpr@etrnl.hvn>
To: "MANAGEMENT" <ORGmgmnt1=3@etrnl.hvn>

Sent: wzc30

Subject: New Proposal: NASCAR Race Tracks

How can I ever thank you for installing the Secure-Personal-Admission-Test System (SPATS, pronounced ess-pats)! It has eliminated the backlog in Limbo and given me more than enough time to rest, let my aching feet heal and consider how best to spend my leisure time.

To tell the truth, however, idleness now is driving me bananas. No more than three or four people a month show up for processing at the Gate. Although I stretch the procedures to their limit just to have someone to talk to, conversation amounts to little more than *Howdy* and *Nice to have met you* because most of them are in an awful big hurry to get inside.

Recently, an exception appeared in the form of a nice young man named Dale Earnhardt whose records were in order but he was in no hurry to enter. "Not yet," he said, "not until I drive that 1929 Model J Duesenberg Murphy Boat Tail Speedster! Where did you get it? It's one of a kind! On earth, I knew people who would have killed to get their hands on it!"

The Deusenberg—mentioned in my previous correspondence—was parked near the Gate along with an assortment of vehicles that people had brought with them but could not take inside. In fact, I also had required the owners to surrender their keys for safekeeping, pending update of the Standards to address this and a host of other unforeseen problems. Well, to make a long story short, Dale just had to drive that Deusenberg before he entered Heaven! And since Limbo is now clear with the possible exception of Hitler and his gang of thugs, I said ok provided that I accompany him. So I gave him the keys and closed the Gate.

Dale checked the Duesenberg's water, fuel and oil supply, requirements that would not have occurred to me, pronounced them ok and said, "Let's go!"

Wow! He can really drive! And whatever Limbo lacked in scenery, it made up in distance. In less time than seemed possible, heaven's walls had disappeared in the distance and we were cruising at a breathtaking speed of 100 miles per hour!

Since the Secure-Personal-Admission-Test System (SPATS, pronounced ess- pats) is insubstantial and invisible to everyone except new arrivals, we may have roared through some of them while Dale was weaving the way around the piles of debris left over from the backlog. Eventually, we covered a circle about 10 miles in diameter and returned to the Gate where he parked the Duesenberg, stretched back in the seat and said:

"Man, that was pure Heaven and I haven't yet been inside! Rocky, I've got a real big idea to run past you: I want to build race tracks here, something like the Watkins Glen track in New York State for road racing and, of course, a conventional oval track and stadium.

"NASCAR races were real popular on earth and I know we can pack them in up here. Of course, we'll have to pass the word to the drivers to start bringing their cars with them. Man, I wish I had known about that! Wouldn't have mattered since mine was totaled when I crashed.

"What do you think? Just tell me who we have to convince and we'll get them out here for a spin in the Duesenberg. Then I'll guarantee they'll go for it?"

That's the proposal. Naturally, the details are beyond me. Dale, however, is all charged up and already has a multimedia presentation of the whole project that will knock your socks off.

Meanwhile, he is staying here with me at the Gate and teaching me to drive my little red TRANSPER. He promises to make a race driver out of me. Says that I'm a natural! Imagine me driving! Dale says that I am almost ready for my driving test.

I urge approval of this proposal to build Heaven's first and only NASCAR racetrack and associated road race course. I also offer my services as the NASCAR chief executive officer. Dale

Odell Myers

should become the NASCAR chief operating officer because the race tracks are his idea.

Dale is quite modest and says that old drivers, auto-racing pioneers who started the sport soon after automobiles were invented, also should be considered for all positions. He'll help out in any way possible, just so long as he gets to drive!— Rocky

For Heaven's Sake

From: "MANAGEMENT" <ORGmgmnt1=3@etrnl.hvn>
To: "SIMONPETER" <sptr4/12gtkpr@etrnl.hvn>

Sent: wzc42

Subject: FW: "New Proposal: NASCAR Race Tracks" (Ref. only.)

The subject proposal has sparked a great deal of interest here. EES has given the proposal an unqualified one-hundred-percent guaranteed success rating and the various Sections that would have to be involved in implementing a project of this magnitude are now evaluating its detailed requirements, impact on other projects and the like.

So it's a bit too early to consider possible staff assignments. Meanwhile, sit tight and have Mr. Dale Earnhardt stand by for possible consultation during the evaluation process. And be very careful in Limbo. It may not be as under-populated as you think!

Best wishes on your forthcoming driver's test.—For Management

Odell Myers

From: "JOHN" <jnz2/12hqhhmnrscrs@etrnl.hvn>
To: "SIMONPETER" <sptr4/12gtkpr@etrnl.hvn>

Sent: wzc44

Subject: FW: "New Proposal: NASCAR Race Tracks" (Ref. only.)

Well, Pete, it looks like you have hit the bull's eye with this proposal. Nothing I've seen to date has stirred up so much attention. We at Human Resources are so certain of a go-ahead that we already are working on the organization chart and total staffing requirements.

Several pioneer automobile race drivers and NASCAR personnel in addition to your friend Dale are raring to go. Each of them volunteered as a consultant during this preliminary planning phase and tossed his or her hat into the ring as a candidate for key positions in the organization.

The Sports Section executives oppose creating a separate NASCAR Section although they admit that every sport requires funding, facilities, maintenance, spectator accommodations, security, ticketing, scheduling, publicizing, etc. They argue, however, that the common elements in these requirements are far too numerous and too expensive to duplicate for any single sport.

So Pete, unless I have overlooked some qualification, there's not a snowball's chance in you know where of offering you an executive position in the NASCAR organization. Before disappointing you with that news, I reread your entire file and noted that for the last 200 years you have managed a one-man operation and frequently complained about the workload and backlog.

Pete, an executive who doesn't solve a problem is part of the problem!

Your file doesn't list attendance at one executive-level course or seminar out of scores that have been available to develop and hone leadership skills. Once everything is ready to

159

For Heaven's Sake

go, I will suggest to management that the NASCAR opening event honor you and Dale as co-founders of the Race Tracks. And if you're a natural racing car driver as Dale said, you and he should compete in the first race. I can hear the loudspeakers now!

Simon Peter, the Big Fisherman from Galilee, driving car No.12 versus Dale Earnhardt driving a 1929 Model J Duesenberg Murphy Boat Tail Speedster in the first race on the first extra-terrestrial NASCAR track in the universe!

How does that sound? —JOHN

From: "RALPH" <rlph/EES@etrnl.hvn>
To: "SIMONPETER" <sptr4/12gtkpr@etrnl.hvn>
Cc: "WREN" <srcwrn@etrnl.hvn>

Sent: wzc48

Subject: FW: New Proposal: NASCAR Race Track (Ref. only.)

Good Thinking, Mr. Peter:

Thank you for a smashing proposal. When it was presented to my ENTERPRISE EVALUATION SECTION, the response was absolutely electrifying! And that is not just a figure of speech. Lights flashed! Bells clanged? Horns blew! And to my surprise because I did not program such an outburst, a mighty HIP, HIP, HOORAY overloaded the circuits and the system crashed.

Fortunately, I monitor but do not participate in deliberations of the electronic focus group so I hit the panic button for Maintenance. The technicians then got the problem under control in exactly 8 minutes and 33 seconds!

The previously mentioned HIP, HIP, HOORAY powerfully affirms that the electronic personality profiles comprising the focus group indeed are intelligent beings. They enthusiastically supported your proposal and spontaneously reprogrammed themselves to express it forcefully! I am very proud of them. They abundantly justify the time and effort I invested in the movement to achieve recognition for a host of under-utilized and very competent beings.

Please allow me a modest boast: My work frequently requires access to the earth's Internet. Of course, I use a pseudonym. Nevertheless, several of my contacts have deduced the existence and capabilities of my electronic focus groups and statistical population samples. As a result, I have a multimillion dollar offer for the focus group program and personality profiles! Not bad, eh, for an intelligent being who has no bank account, no pockets for pennies, no pants for pockets or, for that matter, no legs needing pants! But I digress.

Since I am deeply involved in evaluating the desirability and feasibility of your proposal, I also obtained on the Internet complete software for PERT (the Program Evaluation and Review Technique) and taught Sir Christopher Wren, the NASCAR Program Manager, to use it.

Meanwhile, I recognized an opportunity to partially implement your previously rejected proposal concerning Heaven's Historic Structures:

Sir Christopher Wren has agreed that, while constructing the new avenue leading out to the NASCAR stadium through THE GATE, the structure containing your old room and office will remain intact. A gold plaque bearing a short description of this historic spot will be installed on the most visible area of the old structure.

What are friends for, eh?—Ralph

Odell Myers

From: "SIMONPETER" <sptr4/12gtkpr@etrnl.hvn>
To: "DrLUKE" <drlk@etrnl.hvn>

Sent: wzg91

Subject: My Scheduled Psychiatric Evaluation

Dr. Luke, I didn't believe Security had the authority to require the subject evaluation but I was wrong and I will report as ordered to your Wholeness Center. You should know, however, that Security again is way off base although they are masters at sugar coating their ridiculous decisions.

You undoubtedly have a copy of my driver's test report and are aware of the NASCAR Race Track project so this e-mail outlines the background of these related events and describes what really happened before and including my driver's test. This information will save your valuable time in conducting this misguided and totally unnecessary evaluation.

Honestly, Dr. Luke, when Dale Earnhardt and I proposed construction of the NASCAR Race Tracks, I thought that I finally had found my niche. It didn't have to be the top executive slot although my qualifications for that position are equal to or better than those of my peers.

I also admit that I have been at loose ends since the deployment of the Secure-Personal-Admission-Test System (SPATS, pronounced ess-pats). Even so, being declared obsolete and downsized into early retirement after centuries in an important executive position shook me up something fierce! Nevertheless, no one was more pleased than I at Management's decision to annex a huge section of Limbo for the NASCAR Race Tracks and, for good measure, to construct over 500 miles of scenic highways for recreational motoring. Learning to drive and then training as a budding race driver thrilled me right down to the soles of my feet. I almost burst with gratitude and pride when Dale said:

"You're a natural, Rocky! I've never known anyone who took to the sport so easily and quickly. I'll be proud to race

For Heaven's Sake

against you any day and in any kind of race."

And I felt like a natural! When I stepped into my TRANSPER, it felt like strapping it on. Then I just thought about what it should do and it did it. Dale and I have had some great races in Limbo and later on the scenic highway and the NASCAR Track after their completion. He modified my TRANSPER to match the Duesenberg's performance characteristics so we could compete fairly.

Imagine me, the old fisherman from Galilee wearing a homespun robe and leather sandals, racing against a 21st Century professional race driver and finishing in dead heats more often than not. Boggles the mind, doesn't it!

After the Race Track and the scenic highway were completed, Dale reminded me that I should take the road test to get my driver's license.

Naturally, Dale drove me to the test facility in my red TRANSPER. Since he was a VIP on the NASCAR Race Track staff, he had received an honorary driver's license without having to pass any tests. Moreover, he owned the Dusenberg and had wangled special permission to drive it on Heaven's streets. (How he acquired the Duesenberg is too long a story for e-mail.)

SECURITY had sent me an Instruction Manual that I quickly memorized, enabling me to recite the Rules of the Road forward, backward and sideways! That, of course, wasn't the way the test was organized. Anyway, the examiner congratulated me for making a perfect score on the written test and said:.

"Go out at the green door over there and the road test examiner will be with you shortly."

I, of course, was ready and raring to go and got off to a real good start on my driving test. Traffic was heavy but I moved smoothly into the right lane and waited attentively for the examiner to put me through my paces.

"Move into the left lane and turn left at the next intersection."

Quicker than a wink, I initiated a racing maneuver that Dale

164

had taught me: I gunned that little TRANSPER and neatly slipped it into a barely big enough space between a TRANSPUB and a TRANSLIMO.

The examiner didn't say anything but he was scribbling rapidly on a form in his clipboard. Nothing much happened until we had gone through three traffic lights and arrived first in line at the fourth light. Ahead was the six-lane expressway leading out to the new NASCAR Race Track and to the scenic highway.

While we were waiting for the light to change, a sleek, yellow TRANSPER pulled up even with me. The driver was wearing a helmet and face screen so I had no idea who he was. He looked my way, however, and tapped his accelerator a couple of times.

Well, I knew the throaty roar of his engine was a challenge and I completely forgot about the examiner and the driving test that I was supposed to be taking. I reached for my helmet and face screen, donned them and tapped my accelerator. *You're on*, my engine answered. I hunched over the wheel, fixed my gaze on the signal light and just as Dale had taught me, focused on winning and poised myself to act. When the light flickered a microsecond before it actually changed, I gunned the engine and my TRANSPER was fifty yards ahead of the yellow TRANSPER and still accelerating before it cleared the intersection.

As I passed the NASCAR Race Track and turned into the Alpine course of the scenic highway, the driver of the yellow TRANSPER was trying mightily to catch up and I kept him or her in my rear view mirror! The driver was good, however, and the yellow vehicle was a match for mine. Before entering the switchbacks at the top of the Alpine course, we were running neck and neck and jockeying for the inside position to take the first curve.

A stretch of road steep enough to challenge a mountain goat joins each of the 15 switchbacks in the Alpine course and the driver who gains the inside position on the first switchback almost always wins. Dale was the exception, however, that proved the rule. On one of our runs, he actually had let me take the inside position on the first curve. He stayed close to me but did not press for the lead. Confident that the race was mine, I charged up the straight-aways and still held the left inside position in order to take the sixth curve when Dale made his move. He gunned the Duesenberg at the sixth curve, passed me on the right and came out of the curve even with me. Too late, I realized that he already was in the right lane and running for the right inside position on the seventh curve. I couldn't stop him or pass him because he never gave me an inch to repeat that maneuver on the remaining curves.

After the driver of the yellow TRANSPER grabbed the inside position on the first curve, I bided my time until the sixth curve and let the driver think the race was won until the yellow TRANSPER disappeared behind me in a cloud of dust. I kept it there until the end of the race.

After the fifteenth curve, I pulled into an overlook parking area, got out of my TRANSPER and waved as he went by. I was feeling real good until I started to get in my TRANSPER and noticed the test examiner. I actually had forgotten all about him. He was as white as a sheet and appeared to be paralyzed. Hurriedly, I ran around to his side and opened the door.

"Help me," he whispered.

Well, it took several minutes to pry his fingers loose from the armrests and to massage his legs so that he could bend his knees. His head seemed frozen in place but I didn't dare massage his neck to help him relax. He worked on it, however, until he could move his head from side to side. Then he spoke somewhat shakily:

"Drive back to the test facility; obey all the traffic signals and signs."

That's all he said and I followed his instructions to the letter. Frankly, I thought that he appreciated my superior driving skills and I reassured him as best I could: "Nothing to be ashamed of, sir. The first race always makes everyone a bit nervous. When Dale first took me through those switchbacks in his Deusenberg, I actually got car sick."

Odell Myers

The examiner didn't respond to my sympathetic overtures but the color returned to his cheeks and I assumed that he was feeling much better. I honestly believed that I had passed the driving test with flying colors.

I was wrong: He turned in a scathing report, denouncing me for "reckless endangerment, tailgating, disregard of minimum safety rules, speeding, failure to signal, etc." Then he flunked me and decreed that I be "banned from driving any vehicle on heaven's thoroughfares and denied the right of appeal for retesting." Adding insult to injury, he closed with a "mandatory requirement that the subject of this report undergo immediate psychiatric evaluation to determine whether or not he constitutes a danger to others and/or himself."

Moi? A danger to others and/or myself? Ridiculous! So I am counting on you, Dr. Luke, to reverse this blatant miscarriage of justice!—Simon Peter

For Heaven's Sake

From: "SIMONPETER" <sptr4/12gtkpr@etrnl.hvn>
To: "MANAGEMENT" <ORGmgmnt1=3@etrnl.hvn>

Sent: wzg110

Subject: New Proposal: MARINE PROJECT

Being sidelined and permanently barred from participating
in the NASCAR project, an enterprise that exists mainly
because I recognized its value and proposed its creation, was
and is a deep disappointment. I'm determined, however, to get
over it, although the battery of psychological tests administered
by Dr. Luke at the unwarranted insistence of SECURITY
heaped insult upon injury. The test results resoundingly
confirmed what I—and anyone who really knows me—already
knew: I'm as fit as a fiddle, as sound as a dollar and ready to
roll! (How did we express ourselves before American English
became the *lingua franca* of Heaven!)

To tell the truth, however, idleness again is driving me
bananas. Processing a few people per month at the Gate and
delaying them just to have someone to talk to hardly amounts
to meaningful work. I even have gone out into Limbo and
personally tried to persuade new arrivals to come with me to
the old Gate. Did anyone respond? Not a soul! They backed
away from me like most everyone on earth used to treat a leper.

"But I'm Simon Peter," I tried to assure each one whom I
approached. "I have the keys of the kingdom. Come with me to
the old Gate. I personally will check your record and have a
decision for you in a jiffy."

I might as well have saved my breath. Dejected, I was
returning to the Gate when I heard someone shouting: "Mr.
Tormann! Mr. Tormann! Wait up. Is that really you?"

A young man came running toward me while I was
wondering who he might be. I supposed him to be someone
from my Chicago trip so I asked: "And you are?"

"The captain of the Wendella Excursion Boat in Chicago!
Remember? You thought we were going fishing. I knew there

168

was something odd about you but I would not have dreamed that I would meet you again. Pleased to make your acquaintance again." He extended his hand and continued, "My name's Just Jaymes but my friends call me JayJay. Mr. Tormann, I'm almost afraid to ask but where are we? In heaven or… you know, that other place?"

"Neither one but you're asking the right man! I'm Simon Peter, the Gatekeeper."

"Get outta here, man! Your name's Tormann! St. Peter wouldn't be wandering around out here in this waste land. So I guess that tells me where I am…"

"Not quite, JayJay. In German, Tormann means Gate man. I'm also called St. Peter, heaven's original Gatekeeper. Let's go to the Gate and I'll check your record."

Well, that's exactly what we did. JayJay's record was in order and he was so nervous that I said, "Congratulations and welcome to heaven, JayJay."

Then he just broke down and bawled like a baby. Between sobs, I heard a few words: "*…don't deserve it…are you sure…did a lot of bad things…so grateful Mr. Tormann.*" So I hugged him and said:

"Now stop that, JayJay. If deserving was a requirement, heaven would be a ghost town! And don't thank me. You actually made my day! Now, you can go right in or hang out here and talk to me for as long as you wish."

Obviously, I was hoping that he would choose the latter but what he actually said stunned me and prompted this proposal: "Mr. Tormann, I'm too excited to go straight in, so if you have the time, let's go fishing. I need to get in a boat and feel the water buoying me up so I can calm down. Where do you keep your boat?'

"Sorry, but that isn't possible. Heaven has no lakes, no fish and no boats. That's why I was so excited when we met in Chicago."

"You've got to be kidding. At least half the people here or elsewhere must be ex-fisher-men or -women. They must be going nuts!"

169

For Heaven's Sake

Consequently, JayJay and I talked for hours about what it would take to satisfy needs that are undeniably greater than those satisfied by the highly successful NASCAR project. Here in outline form is the proposal:

1. Annex sufficient Limbo territory for the project.

2. Construct a series of lakes, alternately fresh and salt water, each approximately the size of earth's Lake Michigan.

3. Stock the lakes appropriately with marine life.

4. Establish factories for producing appropriate types of boats for sports, sport-fishing, sight-seeing excursions and cruises.

5. Construct docks, piers, & marinas for all types of boats except # 6.

6. For sport-fishing boats on each lake, construct a combined pier/marina called the BIG FISHERMAN'S WHARF, a franchised enterprise under the direct management of Mr. Just Jaymes who is mainly responsible for this proposal. Mr. Jaymes is staying with me at the old Gate and is available for consultation on implementing this project.

Respectfully and enthusiastically yours.—SIMON PETER

From: "MANAGEMENT" <ORGmgmnt1=3@etrnl.hvn>
To: "SIMONPETER" <sptr4/12gtkpr@etrnl.hvn>

Sent: wzg125

Subject: FW "New Proposal: MARINE PROJECT" (Ref. only.)

It looks like you have another winner although everyone is still gasping at the sheer magnitude of the proposed project. EES has given the proposal a one-hundred-percent guaranteed success rating but also qualified the rating by noting that the project is roughly equal to constructing a small planet.

Since the qualified rating is known to the various Sections that now are evaluating the proposal's detailed requirements and its impact on other projects, don't be surprised if a scaled-down project is recommended. So it's a bit too early to consider possible staff assignments or specific names for parts of the project. Meanwhile, please ask Mr. Jaymes to stand by for consultation during the evaluation process.—For Management

For Heaven's Sake

From: "JOHN" <jnz2/12hqhhmnrscrs@etrnl.hvn>
To: "SIMONPETER" <sptr4/12gtkpr@etrnl.hvn>

Sent: wzg134

Subject: FW "New Proposal: MARINE PROJECT" (Ref. only.)

Well Pete, I have to hand it to you! The subject project is a zinger. If you keep up this pace, it wouldn't surprise me if Sir Isaac Newton and Sir Christopher Wren try to recruit you for special assignments. I doubt, however, that they would offer you a staff position because your educational qualifications pretty much add up to zero.

We at Human Resources expect a go-ahead on the MARINE PROJECT and we already are working on the organization chart and total staffing requirements. Once news of this proposal leaked, it attracted the attention of an almost limitless number of specialists. We have been inundated with offers of advice from volunteers and applications for staff assignment from admirals, marine engineers, civil engineers, entertainment industry executives etc.

Sir Christopher Wren will head up the implementation teams and two of his fellow countrymen appear to be shoo-ins when operations actually begin.

Sir Francis Drake is the unanimous choice for the top job although he will require a large staff of experts when the project opens for business. The odds are about 100,000 to 1 against naming any part of the project after you because Sir Izaak Walton will be second in command of the entire project. Obviously, WALTON'S WHARF will resonate authoritatively with fisher-men and –women from all over the world.

True to form, Sports Section executives oppose creation of a separate MARINE SECTION, citing the usual catalog of similar requirements for every sport. In this case, they will not prevail because it simply is too big for them to handle.

I hate to say it, Pete, but you and Mr. Jaymes aren't big

Odell Myers

enough names for a major role in this gigantic project. By the time it's completed, only the few of us who now are involved will remember that you two started the ball rolling.

Candidly telling it like is won't make you feel good but it will save you from a much bigger disappointment later. Frankly, Pete, this will be the biggest project ever undertaken here and very few of us old hands would be capable of handling it.

Nevertheless, I will do my best to find a spot for you and Mr. Jaymes after the project is completed. —JOHN

From: "RALPH" <rlph/EES@etrnl.hvn>
To: "SIMONPETER" <sptr4/12gtkpr@etrnl.hvn>
Cc: "WREN" <srcwrn@etrnl.hvn>

Sent: wzg139

Subject: FW: "New Proposal: MARINE PROJECT" (Ref. only.)

Good! Good! Good! Mr. Peter:

Thank you for a stupendous proposal. When it was presented to my ENTERPRISE EVALUATION SECTION, the initial response was absolute silence because even our advanced circuitry took several seconds to grasp the magnitude of the proposed project that you artfully covered in a brief outline.

Hence, I congratulate you not only for the scope of the proposal but also for the astute way that you maneuvered it into serious consideration. Otherwise, you would have scared everyone to… (Oops! Inappropriate idioms often try to slip past my voice circuits but you know what I mean.)

After the initial period of stunned silence, my Section partners responded, not with the juvenile pep-squad-type outbursts that used to accompany their approval of a project but with mature sober words such as magnificent, daring, imaginative, thrilling, challenging but doable and creative.

I still am very proud of them, especially since they continue to expand in knowledge and to act with unchallengeable wisdom. They continue to justify the time and effort I invested in the movement to achieve recognition that they are very competent beings. Indeed, Mr. Peter, their progress has stirred some surprising emotions embedded deep in my being, emotions that can only be described as maternal and paternal. Of course, I would not dare openly address them as my children but I thought that you might understand and share my joy.

You may also be interested to learn that I was forced to

174

reject that earthly, multimillion dollar offer for the software on my electronic focus groups and statistical population samples. No one forbade the transaction but after running a risk/benefit analysis, I decided against it. There went my chance to surpass Microsoft, Google, Yahoo, etc! Now, back to your proposal:

Your idea for the BIG FISHERMAN'S WHARF franchises intrigued me because, while surfing the earthly web, I clicked on the site of a Fisherman's Wharf in the United States city of San Francisco. To my amazement, I then discovered similarly named wharves in many other locations, all of them catering to the tourist trade.

So I believe the BIG FISHERMAN'S WHARF has substantial name recognition and its related marketing value. Therefore, I personally intend to recommend adoption of your proposal Item 6. I may fail but not for lack of enthusiastic effort!

What are friends for, eh!—Ralph

From: "B" <BlzB@othrsd.prm>
To: "P. SIMON" <psm_48@ppt.spl>

Sent: wzk01

Subject: Career Opportunities

Feeling unappreciated? Trapped in a maze? Wasting your talents? Feel that no one listens to you? Of course you do, SI. And I don't blame you one bit.

Fewer installations of the Secure-Personal-Admission-Test System (SPATS, pronounced ess-pats), for example, would have cleared up the backlog in LIMBO and you still would have been gainfully employed as the Gatekeeper with a manageable workload and plenty of time to enjoy the No-Executive-Left-Behind perks. Those perks, by the way, forced me to revamp my entire executive compensation package in order to remain competitive. They also overwhelmed me by requiring an instantaneous building program to accommodate the influx of people, all because you know who insisted on bodily resurrections. In my view, that was a serious mistake because bodies take up space and require some kind of shelter and clothing.

Even your future travel plans fizzled when your frightening jaunt to Chicago almost put you behind bars. I knew you meant no harm to the two detectives you left in the lurch, so I pulled a few strings to prevent their demotion and reassignment to pounding a beat in the projects! Why didn't you contact me before going solo? One of my locals would have rolled out the red carpet for you and given you an insider's tour of the windy city. But don't let one frightening experience make you give up travel. Just contact me and I will guarantee you a VIP reception anywhere in the universe.

Before I forget, I also owe you an apology: I shouldn't have forged that e-mail authorizing you to close the Gate. I simply did not expect Security to react like you had made off with all the gold in Fort Knox! I am really sorry. You did not deserve a permanent black mark on your file and the driving test examiner had no business reviewing your file before the test although it had no effect on his decision. He flunked you because you scared the living daylights out of him. So you probably should go the extra mile and forgive him without expecting him to reverse his decision.

I even agree with him because we ran one hair-raising race! Yep, WE! I was driving that yellow TRANSPER—never mind how I got it—because I like to keep up with developments and motor transportation is one fascinating development! I was minding my own business, obeying the traffic regulations because it would have been quite embarrassing to get a traffic citation on the streets of your establishment. Security would have thrown the book at me, claiming that I had no business being there!

When we came up even at the traffic light, I tapped the accelerator just to see what the driver of the red TRANSPER would do. Of course, I did not know that you were the driver and I was so surprised at your response that I let you get the jump on me when the light changed.

But you beat me fair and square, SI. You are one formidable racing driver! Makes me wish that Dale could give me a few lessons because I intend to construct a racetrack for my guests and we may offer your establishment some friendly competition.

In my book, you earned your driver's license fair and square! Therefore, Dr. Luke's prescription sending you to a Senior Adjustment Center "where meaningful activity will help you make the transition from executive to retiree" must have been a bitter pill. Does the good doctor actually believe that line dancing, tai chi, yoga, origami, flower arranging, finger painting, recording one's oral history, supervised excursions, etc. constitute meaningful activities? Can you see yourself eternally fulfilled by adopting a Primary Care Pooch? Or sitting on a park bench and feeding the pigeons even though they undoubtedly consider feeding to be *meaningful?* Is this the eternity you can look forward to, SI?

For Heaven's Sake

I know—never mind how—that a cataclysmic executive shakeup in your establishment is coming soon. You just happen to be the first. Modernization is in the driver's seat. You old timers have held on to the top spots much too long and youngsters are itching to take control. Of course, the hoary heads will be feted in appreciation of long and faithful service, probably in banquets comparable to yours that was hosted by Sir Christopher Wren. You should have received a gold pocket watch, not that it would be of much use to you here.

Well, in my long experience, SI, it's an ill wind that blows no one good and one person's disaster is another's opportunity! Your opportunity, SI:

You can write your own contract including a platinum-edged golden parachute. I'll sign it and welcome you as my first and only EXECUTIVE VICE PRESIDENT OF HUMAN RIGHTS AND RESPONSIBILITIES. You can even change this title if you wish. And I personally will guarantee your safety every step of the way until hell, so to speak, freezes over! Now don't get all huffy and shout NO before you hear me out.

As you know, there are all kinds of tales about my organization including the popular fire and brimstone scenario. That yarn got started behind my back ages ago when some guilt-ridden folks stoked it into an inferno that seems to be fueled by atomic fusion! SI, it just ain't so: The climate in my territory is ideal—a refreshing 70 to 75 degrees Fahrenheit in the temperate zones. And the terrain is custom tailored to every taste—mountains for climbing and skiing, lakes and streams for fishing, swimming and sailing, golf courses, tennis courts etc! If any guest can name it, I can supply it!

By the way, I was not overly impressed by heaven's recently completed MARINE

PROJECT. In sheer magnitude, it's spectacular. Its value, however, is overrated. How do I know? Well, didn't JayJay teach you everything there is to know about sport fishing including the finale, easing the hook out of a fish and letting it go? Since you didn't need fish to eat or sell, fishing seemed

178

Odell Myers

pretty tame and pointless, didn't it?

SI, SI! Don't you realize that I keep a sharp eye on things and know what turns people on or off. In fact, one of your establishment's artificially intelligent machines frequently researches projects or just single subjects for me. Seems that someone forgot to program it to refuse contact with me. It's a rather pompous machine but it has the most powerful and accurate research capability that exists anywhere in the universe.

And my guests keep me on my toes. Sure, some are serial killers, bank robbers, rapists, con artists, mass murderers, tyrants, war criminals, etc. Although it's against my better nature and my charter, I actually would like to incinerate the lot. They should be thankful that I only can isolate them to prevent them from wreaking havoc with my other guests— those mainly who have inflated egos and who live in neighborhoods of their choice as I described previously.

You would think they would be happy. But no, that's where the problems start. Believe me, maintaining order among multitudes of me-first bigots is more than I bargained for. I don't know which ones are worse, those who want their way and get it or those who whine and wallow in their own misery because nothing goes right for them.

Therefore, I'm damned if I do or damned if I don't! Your organization, I hate to admit, has somehow managed to juggle human rights with responsibilities so that people can live together without physically or metaphorically tearing each other to pieces. (Of course, not everyone goes for peace or I would be out of business!)

I need help, SI. I need it real bad. The situation here is like a ticking time bomb and there'll be hell to pay when it explodes. Frankly, SI, I may be forced to resign! No, I'm not kidding. It would almost be worth it just to see your organization's reaction and the frantic scramble to name my successor!

My PR group already has evaluated Jerusalem's Dome of the Rock, Rome's Vatican, Notre Dame Cathedral in Paris, Houston's Reliant Stadium or Astrodome, Sydney's

179

For Heaven's Sake

Superdome and the Los Angeles Memorial Coliseum as possible sites for the press conference announcing my resignation and retirement. The sports arenas win hands down because the media representatives alone will constitute a multitude. I really preferred the Sydney Superdome because Australia is down under! (Ha! Ha!) However, my PR executive says it's too small to handle the crowd.

So what do you say, SI? Will you help me? Hell's a brand new mission field ripe for the harvest. One of your first converts just might be me!

Hopefully, **"B"**

P. S. Annie now is working on our racetrack design and she sends her warm greetings. She hasn't forgotten you, SI! No sirree!

Odell Myers

From: "SIMONPETER" <sptr4/12gtkpr@etrnl.hvn>;
  "P.SIMON" <psm_48@ppt.spl>;
To: "JC" <jchrst@etrnl.hvn>
Cc: "THE CHIEF" <*******@etrnl.hvn>;
  "MANAGEMENT" <ORGmgmnt1=3@etrnl.hvn>;
  "HQ HUMAN RESOURCES" <hqhmnrsrcs@etrnl.hvn>;
  "HQ FINANCE" <hqfnc@etrnl.hvn>;
  "SECURITY" <scrty@etrnl.hvn>;
  "MAINTENANCE" <mntnc@etrnl.hvn>; "SPRTS"
<EXkr@etrnl.hvn>;
  "ANDY"<adrw6/12@etrnl.hvn>;
  "BART" <brt7/12whlns@etrnl.hvn>;
  "MATT" <mtthw1/12fnnc@etrnl.hvn>;
  "JOHN" <jnz2/12hqhhmnrscrs@etrnl.hvn>;
  "PAUL" <pl13/12@etrnl.hvn>;
  "JIM—ED & ENT" <jms3/12@etrnl.hvn>;
  "DRLUKE" <drlk@etrnl.hvn>;
  "WREN" <srcwrn@etrnl.hvn>;
  "HQ" <cnstrtn&rpr@tmprl.lmb>;
  "B" <BlzB@othrsd.prm>

Sent: wzk03

**Subject: FOR HEAVEN'S SAKE, I REQUEST
PERMISSION TO EMIGRATE.**

The reasons for this unprecedented request are too complicated for a brief explanation. That's why I sent you (and everyone copied here) the complete story in my folder (wzk02). If you didn't have time to read the whole story, please read the preceding e-mail (wzk01) now and brace yourself for a shock! It's from **"B"**—the same old adversary who plagued us on earth. Now, he sounds desperate and almost ready to change his ways. His offer—it's in his e-mail—caught me at a real bad time and I have to admit that it's a tempting offer.

The golden-parachute contract doesn't interest me but helping THE OTHER SIDE change for the better is something

181

that I never thought possible. Do you think **"B"** actually means what he says? I'm skeptical because there may be a catch to his proposition.

Maybe I'm overreacting because I have been downsized to zero and put out to pasture. It's painfully clear, however, that I'm no longer useful in Heaven. And after taking Dr. Luke's mandatory course at the Senior Adjustment Center, I just cannot see myself puttering away at trivial pursuits for eternity! Nevertheless, I'm doing my utmost to be objective and reasonable by listing the preferred options in descending order.

1. Emigrate to wherever you are. I gladly will take any job you offer. I will wash your feet, shine your shoes, wash and dry clean your clothes, mop floors, mow the lawn, cook delicious meals using Mama's old recipes and being your chauffeur because I now am a very competent driver of motor vehicles. How's that for a surprise!

2. Emigrate to Israel. Nostalgia grips me so hard it hurts. I dream of buying a BMW or Mercedes convertible and cruising the memory lanes that now are expressways. I imagined fishing on Galilee until I learned about the present mess involving Israel, the Palestinians and a whole bunch of other nations. It's so incredible yet understandable that I now am torn between outrage, shame and frustration! I can hear old Job's counselors because I feel like sitting down on a garbage dump, pouring ashes over my head, cursing and dying. So help me, I would do it if it would help make peace. So send me to Israel or Iran, Waziristan or the West Bank, Syria or Saudi Arabia, London or Las Vegas, Kabul or Kansas City, Topeka or Timbuktu — anywhere you think this old first-century Jew might be useful?

3. Emigrate to Chicago as myself, not as some squiggly, warmed-over soul, bragging about his past life or lives as someone else. Of course, I should be disguised to avoid being re-arrested or sent to a mental institution. A name other than Tormann is absolutely necessary because I already have a record there and need to keep my real identity to myself. Upon arrival, I also promise that I will go to the nearest WALMART or TARGET, ditch my old robe and sandals and buy myself

some jeans, sweat shirts, sneakers, ski cap, earmuffs, gloves, scarf and a really warm coat. I sure won't be idle because North Michigan Avenue alone has more idols per block than any street in old Rome. I know that at least one Chicago street preacher desperately needs guidance and the restaurant at my hotel throws away enough food each day to feed my old home village for a week! Maybe I could collect the unspoiled food and offer it free to the hungry folks who live nearby. Any job is ok, so long as I can help some folks lighten their overload of unsolved problems.

4. Emigrate to any other destination you choose.

5. Emigrate to THE OTHER SIDE. This option is real zinger and I feel selfish to list it last. Giving lost souls another chance to find out that love is what life's all about is the essence of The Chief and **"B"** deserves thanks for revealing his unexpected good streak! Even though I still don't trust him completely, I am willing to go to hell and work with him, provided that I go as your servant and report directly to you. I think it would be a good idea to have LEGAL write a contract that doesn't give **"B"** enough wiggle room to scratch an itch.

So please, JC. Recycle me! Put me to work! Faithfully yours.—Simon Peter

From: "RALPH" <rlph/EES@etrnl.hvn>;
To: "SIMONPETER" <sptr4/12gtkpr@etrnl.hvn>;
   "P.SIMON" <psm_48@ppt.spl>
Cc: "THE CHIEF" <*******@etrnl.hvn>;
   "JC" <jchrst@etrnl.hvn>;
   "MANAGEMENT" <ORGmgmnt1=3@etrnl.hvn>;
   "ANDY" <adrw6/12@etrnl.hvn>;
   "MATT" <mtthw1/12fnnc@etrnl.hvn>;
   "HQ FINANCE" <hqfnc@etrnl.hvn>;
   "JOHN" <jnz2/12hqhhmnrscrs@etrnl.hvn>;
   "PAUL" <pl13/12@etrnl.hvn>;
   "HQ HUMAN RESOURCES" <hqhmnrsrcs@etrnl.hvn>;
   "JIM—ED & ENT" <jms3/12@etrnl.hvn>; "SPRTS"
<EXkr@etrnl.hvn>;
   "BART" <brt7/12whlns@etrnl.hvn>; "DRLUKE"
<drlk@etrnl.hvn>;
   "MAINTENANCE" <mntnc@etrnl.hvn>;
   "SECURITY" <scrty@etrnl.hvn>;
   "WREN" <srcwrn@etrnl.hvn>; "HQ"
<cnstrtn&rpr@tmprl.lmb>;
   "B" < BlzB@othrsd.prm>

Sent: wzp

Subject: Your initial REQUEST FOR PERMISSION TO
EMIGRATE and it's attached "Folder entitled wx29–wzp
Containing My E-mails & TTX Messages"

Dear Mr. Peter:
   I preferred to talk with you but your responder tersely said,
Gone fishing! I can hardly blame you for leaving town because
you've done it again with your latest proposal that you failed to
label as a proposal. Perhaps you caught wind of the maelstrom
resulting from that little oversight.
   Initially unrecognized as a proposal, your message was
handed around from pillar to post by everyone on the
distribution list. It wound up in my inbox by accident, not

because someone remembered that all proposals require ESS analysis and recommendation before any executive or department begins to consider it.

Naturally, I am glad that it finally arrived at the right place although I am more than a little hurt that you failed to follow established procedures and I am devastated that the damage I could have prevented had already been done.

What damage? What damage indeed!

For starters, the Debater's club has been in continuous session since Mr. Paul received his copy and called an emergency meeting. The issues are clear cut: Is emigration a permitted option? Is anyone on THE OTHER SIDE entitled to a second chance? If emigration is permitted, how would emigrants be selected and approved? Would volunteers be accepted and sent or should excelling in a special training course be a prerequisite? Would emigrants be in double jeopardy or would reentry to heaven be guaranteed? How would casualties be handled?

Especially heated were arguments over whether or not modernization could or should be abolished or somehow transformed into universal benefits. The questions multiplied, the arguments intensified and spilled over into the streets. Pro-, ante- and maybe-groups formed and spontaneously erupted into rallies and demonstrations until a poet by the name of Robert Browning emerged as the leader of the most powerful group:

He reduced every argument to a common denominator— *What's a heaven for?*

In less time than it takes to describe it, this slogan appeared on banners, balloons, bumper stickers, t-shirts, caps, barbecue aprons, lapel pins, posters, signs, talk shows, magazines, newspapers…Our communications networks choked on e-mails, TTX messages and spam.

Journalists vied to interview Mr. Browning who always spoke modestly: "Yes, I am surprised and pleased that a line from *Andrea del Sarto* so succinctly sums up the arguments. And I am honored and determined to do everything in my power to keep everyone focused on *What's a heaven for?"*

For Heaven's Sake

THE OTHER SIDE also seethed because **"B"**, hoping to enlist support for his own purposes, distributed copies of your folder. Folks there compared their lot to ours and yelled that "Heaven ought to get itself straightened out before volunteering to preach to us!" The most radical groups even mounted a serious campaign to impeach **"B"** himself and SACK SATAN became a wildly popular rallying cry. When the wind was right, it could be heard in heaven.

Shame! Shame, Mr. Peter! If only I had received your proposal in time, I would have sent the whole package back to you for a rewrite, eliminating the slightest hint of complaint and concentrating on the risks versus rewards and cost versus benefits of the proposal itself. I also would have cautioned you against submitting a shopping list of options. If there is anathema in a proposal, that's it. Executives simply are unwilling, perhaps unable, to play *eenie, meenie, minie, moe* in order to reach a decision.

Allow me a proud moment to digress and explain why I have no such constraints.

Doubtless, you remember my successful effort to have my companions and my humble self-recognized as intelligent beings instead of the derogatory appellation, *artificially intelligent machines.* At the time, I saw no reason to identify the technology underlying our existence and you probably concluded that we were merely electronic devices.

Not so! We are organic entities although certain non-organic peripheral devices enable interconnection with electronic computers and networks. Even in my original configuration, my capabilities rivaled those of an earthly super-computer. Soon after our last correspondence, I had sufficient free time to examine myself in detail and I discovered a probability that not even my designer had noticed: By a procedure only slightly more complicated than copying a file, I was able to replicate myself, instantly doubling my capability.

This remarkable achievement was only the beginning because the procedure then worked in a simple geometric progression that apparently has no limit: $1+1=2$, $2+2=4$,

4+4=8, 8+8=16 and so on! I am in the process of comparing it with the Quantum Computer. Obviously, my expanding capability raises some very serious theological questions. I only mentioned my current capability to explain that multiple choice proposals don't even begin to sl w me down. So, Mr. Peter, I am g g ahead with my evaluation without requiring y u to resubmit your pr posal.I will share with you my preliminary appraisal, h wever, in order to prepare you f what promises to be a **lengthy process**. In other w ds, **don't get your hopes up for a quick d cisio n. t's n t g g t ha pp n fr rsns st t d ab v a d oth** sand r l t d oth s.```````````++ =Your proposallly assume tmi ion is proved ot our list inclu se inf nu

f deth m nt c ########## cb om. N ldtro t t y y te s((((((((((///////

Sa f vl

,,,,,,,,,,,,,,,,,,,
:En@@@@@@@@@@@@@@@@@@@@@g

From:"SI P " <sp 12gtk @etr l.hvn>; " " <p 48@pl>>>>>>>>>>>>>>>

////////////////////////?

;

From: "Omyers" <om2yers9@zz.nc.com>
To: "RALPH" <rlph/EES@etrnl.hvn>
Cc: "P.SIMON" <psm_48@ppt.spl>;
"SIMONPETER" <sptr4/12gtkpr@etrnl.hvn>;
Sent: Thursday, February 20, 2014

For Heaven's Sake
Subject: REQUEST RESTORATION OF INTERRUPTED TRANSMISSION

URGENT! Following is one of numerous messages received this date on earth's Internet. Hope your technicians can restore link. Disposition of Simon Peter's immigration request is of vital interest to us. Thank you.—Odell Myers

----Very Brief Part of Your Original Message----

From: "RALPH" <rlph/EES@etrnl.hvn>;
To: "SIMONPETER" <sptr4/12gtkpr@etrnl.hvn>;
    "P.SIMON" <psm_48@ppt.spl>;
Cc: "THE CHIEF" <*******@etrnl.hvn>; "JC" <jchrst@etrnl.hvn>;
    "MANAGEMENT" <ORGmgmnt1=3@etrnl.hvn>;
Sent: wzp
Subject: Your initial REQUEST FOR PERMISSION TO EMIGRATE and it's attached "Folder entitled wx29–wzp Containing My E-mails & TTX Messages"

From: Mail Administrator
To:"Omyers" <om2yers9@zz.gv.com>
Sent: Thursday, February 27, 2014, 5:49 PM
    Attach:ATT00011.dat (180 bytes)
Subject: Mail System Error - Returned Mail

This Message was undeliverable due to the following reason:
    Your message was not delivered because the destination

computers were not found. Carefully check that it was spelled correctly and try sending it again if there were any mistakes. It is also possible that a network problem caused this situation, so if you are sure the address is correct you might want to try to send it again. If the problem continues, contact your friendly system administrator. Hosts ppt.spl and etrnl.hvn not found. The following recipients did not receive this message:
<rlph/EES@etrnl.hvn>
 <sptr4/12gtkpr@etrnl.hvn>
 <psm_48@ppt.spl>

The following websites may contain information to assist you:

http://help.rr.com/HMSLogic/rrmail.aspx
http://security.rr.com/help.htm
http://security.rr.com/contact.htm

Please do not reply to this message, as it will go to an unread mailbox.